Forever Old, Forever New

A Novel

Forever Old,
Forever New

A Novel

Daniel Hill Zafren

Published by Time Treasures Books, Goose Creek, South Carolina
www.timetreasuresbooks.com

ISBN 13: 978-0-9833042-7-2

Printed in the United States of America

Cover and interior by Susan Newman Design Inc.

Then spake my friend: "Thy words are
    true;
        Forever old, forever new," ...

— John Greenleaf Whittier,
    "The Chapel of the Hermits"

BOOK ONE

Dedication and Direction

O, *let the solid ground*
    Not fall beneath my feet
Before my life has found
    What some have found so sweet!
Then let come what come may;
What matter if I go mad,
I shall have had my day.

Let the sweet heavens endure,
    Not close and darken above me
Before I am quite sure
    That there is one to love me!
Then let come what come may
To a life that has been so sad,
I shall have had my day.

— Alfred Lord Tennyson

ONE

A popular belief is that before one dies the life lived passes before the person's eyes. To determine if it has been a good and full life, one must dwell on all of the events and people having an affect on it. A brief look barely seems adequate to reach a definitive decision. A detailed scrutiny is necessary to figure out what obstacles arose along the way and whether such were overcome, were overbearing, or were compromised. Then there are the situations, large and small, that led to any success or happiness, or which ended in disappointment. Even just the significance and reaction to any letdowns could prove arduous to judge. Some, undoubtedly, became major or minor regrets along the way. The impact of any regrets also requires extensive introspection. People, good and bad, who influenced feelings and behavior are additional factors. Some would be major and some minor characters in the life play. Thrown into that mix are effects, obvious or subtle, fawned by society and history. All of this points to the irrefutable fact that life is complicated, a good reason to surmise that few of us fully understand it all. And, how many really do not care to understand it? How many just ride along the crest of the wave and let it take them wherever it winds up? How many have the desire and fortitude to change direction if they could?

Madeline Ponte was not facing death, but she often waded through the muddy waters of examining her own life and destiny. She liked to think that such immersion added intellectual and emotional depth to the poetry she wrote. Further inspiration to create poetry came from the spellbinding awe of the works of the great poets upon the early discovery of the majesty of those masterpieces.

Madeline was an unabashed romantic. It was primarily her state of mind that a basic goodness resided in most people and that the beauty of nature had to be respected to be appreciated. Most of all, it was the belief that love was the crowning achievement of a fragile life.

The family came to America from France when Madeline was seven, just at the age when she fluently spoke French and English that her parents taught her and delivered with an entreating French accent, a trait still maintained. Both parents worked for a French magazine covering world events published in Paris and had been transferred to the United States office of the magazine located in New York City which covered developments at the United Nations. They lived in a small apartment on the East Side, and Madeline was in her glory once she was old enough to discover the New York Public Library. From that moment there was little doubt she would become a librarian.

Soon after the family came to New York, the parents found out about the Ethical Culture Society of New York and became active members. Ethical Culture is a religion based on ethics, not theology, whose mission is to encourage respect for humanity and nature to create a better world. Members are committed to personal ethical development in their relations with others and in activities involving social justice and environmental stewardship. A membership meeting was held each Sunday and speakers would expound on the humanistic approach to living, as well as on our culture and family relations. Members were encouraged to add their personal view points and experiences. Often the meeting hall was filled with laughter or tears.

Madeline went to the Ethical Culture School from elementary through high school. She was called Maddie there early on and that stuck with her since then. Having so much in common with the other students, Maddie had an abundance of friends and many she still kept in touch with her through emails, letters, and telephone calls. A high proportion of her school friends went on to productive lives in the arts, sciences, and business.

Being cute, petite, and vivacious, Maddie had her share of boyfriends throughout the school years. While she enjoyed their company and it was satisfying having a date at all of the special school functions, none found that special place in her heart. It prompted a certain longing, almost akin to a form of emotional loneliness. An early poem she wrote vented her thoughts.

When will my love come along?
Will it be when I least expect it?
Will it be when I seek it out?
Will it be in the bright sunshine?
Will it be during a steady rain?
I will know it when it is there.

Where will my love come along?
Will it be along a walkway?
Will it be crossing the street?
Will it be at a busy cafe?
Will it be between rows of books?
Will it be at the crossroads between here and there?
The place will really be unimportant.

When and where consumes my mind,
  As my heart races in anticipation;
Answers are there for me to find
And I will grasp them without hesitation.

Another thing Maddie believed was that poets did not have ordinary dreams. Nocturnal travels were to exotic mind places spurning special feelings to be captured by the pen and harbored in the heart. It gave further impetus to the thought expressed by Edgar Allan Poe that perhaps all of life is but a dream within a dream.

She received her library science degree at Columbia University, graduating at the head of her class. She had dated Henry Foster for nearly two of those college years, but a certain closeness was evasive and she had not been totally satisfied with the relationship. Perhaps it was his consuming interest in the physical aspects of a man and a woman which eventually let her to break away from him. She knew there had to be more, much more. Her intellectual aspect was such a strong part of her human appetite.

Because of her class standing and positive interviews, she was able to get a job as an Assistant Librarian for Collections at Blantyre University, a picturesque college in New England rated among the top institutions of higher learning in the nation. Part of its high academic reputation was due to the substantial library holdings and its knowledgeable staff. Without a car, she lucked into getting one of the furnished faculty town houses within walking distance of the Library as well as to the small college town in the other direction.

Since she was now established on her own and on a career path, her parents decided to move back to Paris. While the stay in New York City had been rewarding and they would miss their only child, the French culture was still their first choice. Some school breaks would be spent in Paris, and since the family had traveled back there numerous times over the years, Maddie considered such as a second home, even though she was now a United States citizen.

It was a rainy day in September as she walked to the Library. The rain had a soothing sound on her umbrella, and Maddie held the raincoat close to her body as an early autumn chill had set in. The newly mowed grass of the extensive grounds filled her nostrils with a pungent aroma. No one else was in view. The students would be starting classes later in the week. All of the sights and sounds were new to her, and her poet's mind celebrated and marked each experience. She felt sorry for all those people who did not linger on such perceptions, as each was a beautiful reminder of the happiness of living the moment. Working and thriving among the books that awaited her, she felt a basic contentment. The love she yearned for would come, of that she was sure. Meanwhile, its absence would not detract from everything else she had. Patience would subdue anxiety.

As she walked, her mind wandered. Often in those instances, since she had read and reread numerous times poems from the giants of poetry, favorite parts of their creations that she had committed to memory would settle in her mind.

We shape ourselves the joy or fear
  Of which the coming life is made,
and fill our Future's atmosphere
  With sunshine or with shade.

The tissue of the Life to be
  We weave with colors all our own,
And in the field of Destiny
  We reap as we have sown.

— John Greenleaf Whittier

TWO

On that same day, Maddie took part in a Library orientation for new faculty members. An outstanding feature of the college was that it attracted superior scholars to teach in the liberal academic environment. The new additions were a continuation of this tradition, and as Maddie scanned their resumes she was duly impressed by the achievements and experience. It was also evident as the session moved on that the newcomers also had an interest in the library for their special fields of interest as well as in general. There were interesting discussions and some pointed questions. Maddie felt honored to give a brief presentation on the status and extent of a portion of the collections.

One of the new faculty members, an attractive young woman with long brown hair and piercing brown eyes, approached her as the session ended. Her voice was mellow and cultured. "I can tell from your accent that you are French. I am French as well, but came here as an infant so I do not have the tell-tale accent." She stretched out her hand. "I am Marie Foundelet."

Maddie grasped the soft hand. "Maddie Ponte. I came here as a child," and she laughed, "Some things you never grow out of."

Marie smiled, "And it is a good thing. Certain qualities should never be outgrown, especially when they are so beguiling."

Maddie remarked pensively, "Hard to keep some things a secret, though."

"Not necessarily a bad thing."

"What subject are you going to teach?"

"English."

"Have you taught before?"

"No, and I didn't even think it would be something I would want to do or even be good at. A string of degrees and publications and the college sought me out."

"Sounds like major accomplishments for one so young."

"I actually look younger than I really am, and I am even undecided whether that is a good thing or not. I suspect that a more mature appearance is a classroom asset. Anyway, young or younger, a restless mind and an unrestrained imagination have made me prolific."

"What sort of publications?"

"A collection of poems and an anthology of short stories. I am hoping while I am here I can work on a full length book."

"I am a poet of sorts. Never tried to get any of them published. They are mainly emotional releases for me. I have read poetry all of my life, primarily the great poets. That was the motivation for me to become a librarian."

"Talk about looking young, you look far too young to have been doing this for long."

"I earned my degree this year."

"So, French Maddie, we are both novices with soft voices and loud ambitions. In the event we do not want others to follow our conversations, we can speak in French. My parents always spoke to me in French and English."

"I'll see if your publications are in the Library so I can read them."

"They probably are because I was not asked to furnish them. But, if not, I'll lend them to you."

"Mighty kind of you."

"And, perhaps, at some point, you can share some of your poems with me."

"I would like that."

"How about a French hug among novices for good luck?"

The two women hugged, and Maddie was optimistic that a comforting and sharing friendship was in the offing. Marie seemed to be a genuine person, reminiscent of her friends at Ethical Culture.

This represented a good omen for a worthwhile tenure at the Library.

Absorbed in her work, the day passed quickly. Careful and exact with her assembling and chronicling collections, venting curiosity along the way in volumes she had not come across before, was a contented activity for her. As she walked back to her housing unit a warm feeling of satisfaction engulfed her.

Once inside, she had a small salad for dinner, skyped her parents in Paris to fill them in on all that was happening, took a shower, and then read part of a book in bed. She fell into a peaceful sleep, believing her vivid poet dreams would reflect her contented state. She had come a long way in her young life. There would undoubtedly be new and divergent paths yet to explore, and that made the prospect of the future that more interesting and exciting.

> *Could I but live again*
> *Twice my life over,*
> *Would I once strive again?*
> *Would not I cover*
> *Quietly all of it —*
> *Greed and ambition —*
> *So, from the pall of it,*
> *Pass to fruition?*
>
> — Robert Browning

THREE

On the next day Maddie was able to locate Marie's publications in the Library's holdings. In fact, there were multiple copies as if the acquisitions people surmised that Marie would assign readings from them to the students. She checked out the poetry and short story books, and was eager to begin reading them when she got home.

In the early afternoon Marie stopped in at the Collections Department. Maddie was working at her desk in the office assigned to her checking items on the computer before another excursion to the stacks.

Marie sat in the chair at the side of the desk. "Hope I am not interrupting."

Maddie moved away from the computer. "The beauty of library work is that breaks are commonplace. They are almost ingrained in the system and often encouraged."

"Good. I won't keep you. I still have lesson plans to go over and complete. It is almost like writing a book. You can't establish a plot unless you have some idea where it is going. You can't fabricate a character unless he or she will be useful to the story. Oh well, that's a different kettle of fish. Speaking of fish, do you like to eat?"

"What true French woman doesn't?"

"Well, I fancy myself as an amateur gourmet chef. My parents loved to cook, and I picked up on that at an early age. I have an apartment above the florist in town. The faculty housing was full. Why don't you come over for dinner on Saturday and we can become better acquainted?"

"That sounds wonderful. What time?"

"Sixish. Is that good for you?"

"Fine. I checked out your books today. Hopefully, I will have read them by then."

"Excellent. Why don't you bring your own favorite poem for me to enjoy."

"I will."

"Is there any food item you dislike?"

"Again, what French woman can turn her nose up on an edible morsel?"

"Dandy. See you on Saturday." With that Marie was gone.

Classes started on Thursday, and the campus was bustling with activity. Much of it had not yet spilled over into the Library, but other librarians told Maddie that the rush would come and stay until the semester breaks and holidays.

On Saturday evening, Maddie started out on the enjoyable walk to town. The fragrance of fallen leaves mingled with smoke from a wood fire coming out of a chimney, a rare treat for a New Yorker. A bottle of French wine was tucked under her arm. She had several bottles in her own kitchen, and it was a pretty good guess that since Marie was French she liked wine. Wine growing and drinking are ingrained in French culture. Legend has it that babies start on wine in their milk bottles. Maddie wondered what wine would taste like through a nipple. Her parents usually had a glass of wine with dinner and when Maddie started high school she was given a small glass at each evening meal. On the trips the family made back to France, often the wine did not come in bottles. The latest harvest, wine nouveau, was transferred from storage containers to stoneware pitchers from which the wine was served at meals.

Maddie had read both of Marie's publications, and she had a sense that there would be much to discuss at dinner. She had a difficult time selecting one of her own poems to take with her for Marie to read. Some of her sentimental favorites might not be substantive enough for a professor to critique. Other than her parents, she had not shown the poems to anyone else. After some deliberation, she chose one of her early poems created when she was in a particularly philosophical mood. Her young life could easily be measured by the time periods corresponding to her intellectual development.

Aged to Perfection

The young have a tendency to squander their youth.
  Perhaps, it is the often fruitless quest for meaning and truth;
As the years pass goals take on a different substance,
  Leaning more to all around comfort and maintenance.

As a young person myself this dilemma is easy to realize,
  Trading for the needs and wants I visualize;
It all translates into goals sent as dreams,
  Knowing full well all is rarely what it seems.

The true secret to aging enjoyment and success
  Is to learn lessons along the way of the process;
A lesson learned adds value to the trip just made,
  It is a foothold on a sturdy foundation laid.

So, bring on old age as I am ready to be there,
  I will make it a science and art form with a flare;
I will journey from youth to a perfect old age time,
  I hope your aging story will be as grand as mine!

The two women hugged, and Marie's eyes widened when she saw the bottle of wine. "I should have guessed. I shall put away the bottle I have out and we'll enjoy it another time."

Maddie smiled. "Sounds like a wine fine time."

Marie giggled. "Sounds like a rhyme wine fine time."

She showed Maddie around the small apartment. There was no separate dining room, just a compact table set up in the living room. The table was set for two and adorned by colorful autumn leaves. "I used leaves I picked up walking from the college yesterday. Fall colors have always fascinated me. If leaves can change to vivid colors the lives of people can change too, hopefully for the better. I don't think we give Nature the credit she deserves."

"Most women fall into that category."

"Amen, or I should say Awomen."

Marie's culinary talent was evident as they feasted on roasted salmon with sauteed fresh vegetables. The wine was the perfect accompaniment. The bread pudding dessert was admittedly the best that Maddie ever had.

After cleaning up they sat on the sofa sipping the remaining wine. Both were completely relaxed. Good food, good wine, and good company are a dynamite combination.

"I read your creative endeavors," Maddie offered. "Your writing talent and ability to pull it off are evident. I am sure your students will be greatly enriched. I must confess, however, I am not an enthusiastic fan of free verse."

"Free verse can be a challenging form of poetic expression. The substance overshadows the form, and it has to be just right for it to work. Thank you for the compliment. I suppose I demand too much from myself, but I would like to do even better. The students may not fully appreciate my driving force."

"You'll do better if you set your sights on that goal. After all, you are young yet."

"You keep saying that. I am no longer a spring chicken. I'm forty-three."

"You sure look younger, and as far as I can tell you have all of the zest of a younger person. Plus, I don't consider forty-three old."

"Another kind observation. I have not had an easy life, and I am surprised it has not taken its toll with, at least, lines in my face and sagging skin."

"I am sorry about that. My life has been smooth sailing, although a meaningful romance has alluded me."

"Ah, a romantic. I should have guessed. I started out as a romantic, but it did not take long for that to be squelched. Too many disappointments followed by a brief bad marriage that changed me and I had to face a new reality."

"Sorry, again."

"Don't be. I guess in most cases it was my fault for one reason or another. A failure to recognize the warning signs can be devastating. I really don't like to talk about it because in a way it is reliving it."

"I can see that. I am content, I suppose, being patient for a love to come along. I have had my share of boyfriends, but there was usually something missing. If I did not believe it will come I would probably be miserable."

"When it does, you can then look for me. Even disappointments have not led me to abandon all hope."

"I'll do that."

"Did you bring a poem?"

Maddie hesitated. "I did. It is one I wrote early on, and I hope you like it." She settled back in the cushion behind her as Marie read it.

Marie read it twice before handing it back. "I like it. You write from the heart and I already know your heart is full."

"Writing poems is a release and a distraction. I don't care if I ever get published. It is my inner self, and I actually prefer to keep it private."

"I can understand that you feel that way now. Some day you may want to share your feelings with others. Perhaps at a later time you can let me read a more recent creation so I can gauge what I call verse growth."

"Sure. What about the book you are going to write?"

"Ah! Right now that is just a wisp of an idea and not fully formed. Perhaps, to echo your journey it will be about a search for love or, at the least, an individual's place in a chaotic world. Whatever it will be it will be a major undertaking and I am not sure I am up to it. Yet, the compulsion is there. It will take many bottles of wine to get it going."

Maddie laughed. "French wine, of course."

"Naturally."

After further delightful discussions, Marie drove Maddie back to her place and came in to look around. It was nice, but she liked being in town, and the lady who owned the florist shop was pleasant and quiet.

All in all, both women basked in this new found friendship. The age difference did not matter in light of the common thoughts and interests. Each harbored the thought that the other was a sister they never had.

I hold it true, what'er befall;
I feel it, when I sorrow most;
'T it is better to have loved and lost
Than never to have loved at all.

— Alfred Lord Tennyson

FOUR

Maddie and Marie went together on Wednesday evening to the new faculty reception at which the arrivals were to be introduced. There were plenty of tea sandwiches and wine, the wine from California which they tolerated. The Dean made a long-winded speech, and it was after ten o'clock by the time it ended. Most of the males in attendance were with their wives, and none of the unaccompanied men approached them for introductions or conversation. Marie introduced Maddie to the other members of the English Department, and Maddie introduced Marie to the Library folks that were there that she had not already met.

Marie was invited to Maddie's place for dinner on Saturday. Maddie was not as proficient as Marie in the culinary department, but lemon chicken had been a family favorite and Maddie had watched her mother make it many times so it was easy to prepare. She hoped Marie would find it passable. Actually, she did enjoy it and they both sipped the French wine Marie brought with her as they cleaned their plates.

They sat in the living room after they washed and dried the dishes, sipping the wine still left in the bottle. Maddie pulled out Marie's book of poetry. She had placed a marker at a certain page. "I was puzzled by a line in the poem about dreams. What do you mean by *Everything is done, nothing is undertaken?*"

"The meaning cannot be taken by the words alone. It fits into the pattern of the entire poem, indicating the scheme that in the world of dreams the dreamer has no control over the specifics of the dream. It is, in effect, all preordained and no amount of effort can change it."

"Dreams have always intrigued me. I believe that because of my poems I have special dreams. Creative people have deeper dreams. I also think they remember more of the dreams than others do."

"Is that because they want to?"

"Perhaps."

"Do you have any repetitive dreams?"

"I have not dreamed the same sequence of events, but the challenging aspects of my life often appear in varying contexts and degrees."

"Such as?"

"Books."

"And romance?"

"Not as often as I would like."

"Do you ever have nightmares?"

"Not in the usual sense. There are times I am in a situation frustrated in not finding an easy way out."

"That can definitely be a nightmare. I have some frightening dreams, times when my very being is threatened, emotionally more than physically."

"What do you think that means?"

"I'm not sure. I like to think it is stress driven, forms of exasperation about my not being able to fully control all of the facets of my life."

"What do you do to alleviate such stress?"

"I write, and I hope the book I undertake will be an escape route. A long walk helps. Drinking wine is a calming element."

"I have been intrigued by Whittier's *Forever old, forever new.* What do you think he meant by that?"

Marie was pensive for a moment. "Prompts thought, doesn't it? Maybe that is what he was trying to do. Perhaps it is a variation of the idea that there is nothing new under the sun. It has been there forever, but it is new when one discovers its existence."

"Like love?"

"Like love."

"Some of your short stories dealt with love. Were they dream inspired?"

Marie was silent for a moment, and Maddie had the impression she had intruded in a place she probably should not have gone. When Marie continued speaking there was a hollowness to the tone of her voice as if a bunch of memories were obliterating her passion. "No, they were steeped in experience. The stories about my love life are, for a lack of a better word, painful. The bad marriage was a difficult time, and there were earlier events that in many ways were more hurtful."

"You don't have to talk about it."

"Writing is a way of releasing pent-up emotions. Talking about it is probably a good thing as well as long as the listening ears are understanding. Memories fade into dreams, and dreams can, I am sure, reshape a memory. Perhaps, one arrives at a place where it is hard to distinguish between the dream and the memory. It probably makes no difference for the anguish it provokes."

Maddie knew she would have to think about this. There are some situations and feelings you cannot fully comprehend unless you have been there yourself. "Again, Marie, please don't talk about it if it is painful. There are many other things we can talk about."

Marie stared off in the distance, and it was an awkward moment before she spoke. "At this point, besides reliving things I am not proud of, I don't want you to think any less of me."

Maddie half chuckled. "What, you don't want me to think you are human after all?"

Marie spoke right up as if she had already decided to confide in her new friend. "When I was in high school I got involved with a bad bunch of girls. I sensed I was heading for trouble but I was impressionable and sought popularity. Poor excuses for putting aside values and heading towards where I did not really want to go." A pause was filled with a sigh. "To gain acceptance and approval, I suppose, and not having the gumption to exert my true self, I was pressured into being sexually active. I did not enjoy it, and I could not take enough showers to cleanse my sensibility. I needed a good kick in the butt, although there was no one there to straighten me out. My parents were detached and had little patience with me. Eventually, I did it on my own and it was no longer important to me when I lost popularity and those half-baked friends." Another pause, another sigh. "It left a scar on my heart. I am hoping the book will be that kick for others. I earnestly believe there can be great power in the ideas conveyed by the written word."

Maddie stretched out her hand and put it on her arm. "I will be anxious to be among those to absorb your thoughts."

"Perhaps you can be my sounding board along the way."

"For sure, and I would love to have your confidence."

"One benefit from bad experiences is that I have a keen sense of whom I can trust. Our friendship is new but old at the same time, shades of Whittier's outlook."

"My experiences are rather limited so I am not sure I can add anything."

"Are you a virgin?"

"Technically, no; emotionally, yes. I have engaged in sex, reluctantly as I assess it, realizing then and emphatically convinced now that without love it is meaningless. There was no enjoyment, no lasting satisfaction."

"Ah, a part of the book in a nutshell. Also, I might add, the painful aspect of being a romantic."

"I am not sure writing about it would have an impact. The state of mind of contemporary society is that you have to try sex to know about it. Peer pressure is prevalent. Temptations and theories are rampant."

"Perhaps, but I feel it must all be said. As you know first-hand, the price of popularity can be far too high."

It was well after midnight when Marie drove back to town. The evening had been enjoyable for both women. An old friendship has the security of knowing the time-tested faith and loyalty are a constant. It has the benefits of mutual participation in events and decisions. Its history is the source of its comfort. Personalities have been nourished and enhanced by the bond. A new friendship brings with it the excitement of the discovery of what a close confidence can bring. An additional hand and understanding to what lies ahead can bring strength of character. The supporting hug softens adversity and magnifies accomplishments.

Rose leaves, when the rose is dead,
Are heaped for the beloved's bed,
And so thy thoughts, when thou art gone,
Love itself shall slumber on.

— Percy Bysshe Shelley

FIVE

With classes in full swing, the University and all of its components were fully active. Students filled the Library to study and jump start present and future assignments. Maddie often had students waiting on her for reference assistance. She imagined Marie was totally engrossed in her teaching responsibilities as there were no visits by her. On Thursday evening she did telephone Maddie with some interesting news. She had been asked out on a date by one of her colleagues in the English Department. He was an older man and had not been at the new faculty reception, but he seemed to be pleasant enough so she accepted the invitation for Saturday night. She promised to call Maddie on Sunday to report on the event.

In the meantime, Maddie had her own happening to dwell upon. A graduate student, Carson Farrell, stopped in to see her twice during the week. He was probably going to be working with the collections daily for his thesis writing and he would require her assistance as well as special access to the collections. She determined he was a serious academic person. His limited conversations with her were intellectually based and he appeared to be in another world. He evidently paid little attention to his personal appearance with an unruly beard, wrinkled clothing that rarely matched, and his old sneakers were about to fall apart. There was no physical attraction, but he certainly was a different kind of person than she was accustomed to. In that sense he was interesting, and his thesis topic required a challenge for her in steering him to the appropriate portions of the collections, some on the obscure side. Even though her name was on the door to her office, he persistently addressed her as ma'am. She arranged for him to get a stack pass from her each time he came to the Library, and the first few times she guided him personally to the areas that would be most useful. The first time he went to the stacks by himself she checked on him a few hours later and found him spread out on the floor between rows of books feeding material into his laptop. He was totally absorbed in his mission and did not notice her, and it confirmed the notion that she had developed that some people do in fact exist in a world of their own.

Maddie spent the weekend alone. She missed having dinner with Marie and the after dinner discussions. Friendship has infinite benefits and pleasures. Yet, being by herself was something she had accepted and always made the best of it. There was perpetually a stack of readings to undertake, poems to work on, long walks to garner the spectacle of nature, and telephone and email contacts with friends and her parents. It was a calm that settled her spirit after a hectic week. For a person secure in habits and thoughts, being alone is a time for reflection and reaping the benefits of its peace. If she had to describe it, such was an inner contentment.

True to her word, Marie telephoned on Sunday evening. Her date had proved barely tolerable as there was really no attraction, and after some easy conversation she became bored with him. As a fallout from all of her prior unpleasant experiences, Marie was the first one to admit that she had developed little patience with relationships that had no reasonable potential. Perhaps her standards were now too high, but to truly satisfy her that is the way it had to be. She proposed they resume the Saturday night dinners with alternate hostings. Maddie readily agreed.

On Monday the weather had turned sharply colder, and Maddie had to bundle up for her brisk walk to the Library. She could tell that country cold was going to take some getting used to. When it had been cold in New York City, she would duck into a shop along the street or enter the nearest subway station. Fortunately, the heating system at the Library was good and she was warmed quickly. The cup of coffee she made with the small Mr. Coffee machine she had in the office helped.

Forever Old, Forever New

Carson knocked on the office door, and she quickly noticed he was not dressed adequately for this cold. He had on what seemed to be a thin shirt covered by a frayed sweatshirt. She motioned him in.

His voice was raspy. "Sorry, ma'am, to get here so early, but I am consumed by a lead I came across in the collections on Friday."

"Don't you know it is quite cold outside?"

He frowned. "I have no time to adapt to the vagaries of the weather."

"Do you have any warm clothing?"

"I have not yet fully unpacked. I have a coat and some sweaters somewhere."

She knew she sounded like a mother but the words came out. "You should be settled in by this time and fully unpacked. You are not dressed right for these temperatures."

"No time and no patience for such trivial things, ma'am."

"Sit for a minute. I will make you some hot coffee. You must be cold. I was half frozen when I got in."

"Mighty kind of you, ma'am," he said in a half stutter. "You already do much for me."

She went out to the water fountain to fill the carafe. As the coffee brewed, both were silent. She studied his long lean face partially obscured by the unruly beard. He was thin, thinner than she thought he should be. In that condition and the scant clothing Maddie guessed there were financial problems, but that was none of her business. Her mother mentioned more than once over the years that if there is a problem you cannot help with then stay clear of it.

She poured the coffee into a paper hot cup. "Sorry. I take my coffee black so I don't keep any sugar or creamer."

"Not a problem, ma'am. I'm not fussy and take it any way I can get it."

Maddie wondered if he was referring solely to the coffee. "There's not supposed to be any food or drinks taken to the stacks, but since it is too early for most others to be around I think it will be alright if you take it with you. I know you are anxious to get started."

She handed him a stack pass and he left quickly, almost as if she threw him out. Normally, it might have bothered her that he did not even thank her for the coffee. However, she had the sense that his troubles obscured a dabbling at manners or protocol, so she just let it slide by as she became engrossed in the pile of work on her desk. It was time-consuming entering data in the computer. Yet, that was one of the evils of the job and she approached it with the resolve she advanced to all things.

A couple of hours passed, and after she helped a few students with information on and access to the collections, she decided to go to the stacks to check on Carson. She also had two books she needed to place in their proper housing which was close to where Carson would be working. Much to her surprise he was not there. She looked around in the area, and still no Carson. She had not seen him leave and he had not turned back in the stack pass as he was supposed to do. There were other ways to exit the Library than by her office and he might even have gone right by her door when she was involved in something else.

It bothered her all day that he had disappeared without saying anything. Between Ethical Culture and the teaching of her parents, she had a basic concern for the well being of other people. The dilemma is in determining whether well being is at risk and if so how much to do about it if you could.

When Carson did not show up the next day for a stack pass, Maddie decided she would try to track him down. Since she was considered a faculty member, she had full access to student records. On her lunch break, she went to the Administration Building and viewed his record. It showed that he was living with an aunt in town but there was no contact telephone number just an address. She wrote the address down, and after work she would walk to town to find the house. It was dark by then, and she stopped at the fire station to inquire where the street was. It was a few blocks from the florist's where Marie had her apartment. She found the street but there was no house matching the number in the record. Maddie's concern and curiosity peaked. She went to the small town police station. One officer was on duty and he checked both the name and address with the records on file there. Nothing existed for either one.

Maddie called Marie from her cell phone telling her she was in

Forever Old, Forever New

town and close by and asked might she stop in for a few minutes. The two hugged when Marie answered the knock on the door. Maddie then blurted out the mystery at hand.

Marie listened intently while the events were being described. She then went to the kitchen to get them both a glass of wine. "Seems to me," she offered after taking a sip, "There are at least two possibilities. First, something evil is afoot. Second, and probably more likely, the fellow has something to hide and wants to be secretive about it."

"I don't know what to make of it. He is registered legitimately as a graduate student on a full scholarship, so why the need to falsify where he is living and with whom? Why would he not want to be found? What could he possibly have to hide?"

"Makes one wonder, doesn't it? Yet, there could be, when you think about it, many reasons one doesn't want to be found. For example, as you describe his dress condition perhaps he is in financial difficulty and is trying to avoid creditors. Then, there is the possibility he is not who he says he is?"

"Why would that be?"

"I really don't know. The writer in me sees all sorts of scenarios, and perhaps this is a genuine mystery."

"Maybe I should ask some of the other people on that street if they know anything about him, the aunt, or even the house number."

"Now your sleuth mode has kicked in."

"If he does not show up for the rest of the week, I'll do that on Saturday."

"Stop here first and I will go with you."

On the next day during her lunch break Maddie went back to the Administration Building to see if there was an emergency contact for Carson in his file. Mary Farrell, identified as Carson's mother, was listed with an Atlanta, Georgia address and telephone number. Maddie tried calling the number and a recording came on saying that the number was not in service. The mystery was becoming more troubling.

Maddie tried a Google search for Carson Farrell and Mary Farrell with no real success. Two Mary Farrells showed up, one in California and one in New Mexico. The connection appeared remote, but she wrote down the information just in case. Maddie also tried the Scholarship Office to see if there was any helpful information there. That turned out to be futile.

No Carson all week, so on Saturday morning Maddie and Marie knocked on the doors to the houses on both sides of the street close to the given Farrell address. None of the occupants had heard of that address or knew anything about a Carson Farrell or his aunt or even Mary Farrell. All of this promised to be a topic of discussion that evening when Marie was to go to Maddie's for dinner.

Marie brought the wine and Maddie made an overstuffed omelet. While eating, there was a recital and discussion of their individual activities for the week. After dinner, as they sat in the living room sipping the remaining wine, the talk turned to Carson.

"I am thinking," Maddie began a bit tentatively, "That I would send a letter to the mother in Atlanta asking her to call me. If she has moved, it should get forwarded to her."

Marie waited until she was sure that was all Maddie was going to say at this point. "I think you should go to the campus police and let them take over from here. Have you considered that there may be something devastatingly wrong and you are putting yourself in danger?"

"I have thought of that, but what if it is just that he had reverted to some situation where his privacy is involved? I would hate to cause him trouble when that is not warranted."

Marie rubbed her chin and then put her hand on Maddie's sweatered arm, "You've started this. Seems to me there is no half way. You need to pull out all of the stops."

Maddie pondered it for a moment. She knew Marie was being reasonable. "I'll send the letter and if Carson does not show up on Monday I'll talk to the police."

I would I could adopt your will,
  See with your eyes, and set my heart
Beating by yours, and drink my fill
  At your soul's springs, – your part my part
In life, for good and ill.

— Robert Browning

It lies not in our power to love or hate,
  For will in us is overruled by fate.

*   *   *   *   *

Where both deliberate the love is slight,
Whoever loved, that love not at first sight?

— Christopher Marlowe

SIX

Monday was another very cold day and there was a heavy frost on the extensive University lawns. As Maddie trudged towards the Library, the vapor from her breath disappeared before her. It reminded her of Carson's apparent disappearance into thin air. She wondered what this week would bring, and since this was a new job she hoped there would not be any further distractions. The rigors of her assignments demanded that she stay focused.

The first cup of hot coffee had a special appeal on a frosty morning, and she hoped Carson wherever he was had a chance to have something hot to drink. She kept glancing up to see if he was approaching her office as he did last week. Being busy helped pass the morning. On her lunch break with determination she headed for the campus police office wondering if this would be her final involvement in the incident.

The Blantyre University Police was headquartered in a small office just inside the main door on the first floor of the Administration Building. A sign on the door said to knock and then enter. There was only one officer in the room sitting at a desk reading a book. Maddie liked seeing that, although she could not see what book it was.

The stocky middle-aged man with graying streaks in a thick head of brown hair looked at her over his glasses. His voice was deep and friendly, "Greetings, young lady. I'm Officer Harry Inman. What can I help you with?"

She had noticed his last name on the name plate on the front of the blue police shirt that also had a University Police patch on the sleeve. "I am Maddie Ponte. I work in the Collections Department at the Library."

He interrupted her. "Glad to meet you, Ms. Ponte. It doesn't take great police work to tell you are French." As he stood up, he was very tall and was wearing jeans.

"It doesn't take great library skills to tell you are only in half a uniform."

He chuckled. "It is usually so empty and dead in here that being in half a uniform is more than should be required."

"This must be the quietest place on campus."

"That it is, and it is what we are used to and what we like. There is not much for police to do in a sort of sanctuary this place represents. Although it was not always like that. There were major campus upheavals here in the late 60s and early 70s and there were even folks back then who thought the place would not survive. Since then, incidents and crime are nearly nonexistent. There is an occasional loud party, or a traffic accident or parking violation now and then. A lost computer would be a busy day for us. With no football or basketball teams, the only crowd event is graduation."

"Sounds boring for one who might like detective work."

"Maybe so, but I like to think boring means we are doing something right. Besides, the perks are exciting enough for me. My children get free tuition. I have twin boys who are seniors and a girl who is a junior in high school destined for an extended academic life at Blantyre. Now tell me why you are visiting? Is a student late in returning a book?"

Maddie thought to herself *If only that were so.* She took a moment before speaking. "You mentioned lost computers. Do you ever find lost people?"

He sat and motioned for her to sit in the chair along side the desk. "I thought you were a student when you came in. You look awfully young, but the older I get the younger everyone else seems to look. Start from the beginning and tell me the whole story."

He was almost fatherly and Maddie felt relaxed. She related all of the events, carefully describing her impressions and even including Marie's suspicions. The narrative ended with her mailing the letter this morning to Mary Farrell in Atlanta.

"Well, young lady," he responded upon completion of her narration, "That is a spellbinding story. I think, however, you may be getting yourself worked up over nothing. Imagination can lead us to all sorts of speculation. First, from my many years here I can attest to the fact that students are unpredictable at best. There can be periods of heavy concentration on studies and then suddenly long periods of slacking off. Second, the academic year is new, and often records are incomplete or contain errors. The number of the house in town could be really different or the house number might be right but the street is wrong. Third, so many other simple explanations might be the case here. For example, he may have gotten sick and left in a hurry and is now recuperating. But, I'll tell you what I will do. I'll make up a report, and we'll check into it as much as we can. There are only three of us here and our jurisdiction is limited strictly to the University. We can work together with the Town Police. Here's a piece of paper. Write down your telephone number and I'll call you if we find out anything. You call me," as he handed her his card, "If Carson shows up or you get an answer from your letter."

"Thank you, Mr. Inman."

"It's Harry to you."

"By the way what book are you reading?"

"Of course, I'm hooked on mysteries. This one my sister in South Carolina sent to me after she met the author at a local literary festival. It is *Network of Death* by Daniel Hill Zafren and it sure has lots of twists and turns so far. I have yet to figure out whodunit. I'll let you borrow it when I am done."

"Thanks, Harry."

Maddie felt a sense of relief as she walked back to the Library. Harry was reassuring, and it was the right thing to do to get him involved. The police have resources at their disposal that others do not have. Anyway, she had taken a positive step and hoped it would be productive.

> Take this kiss upon the brow!
> And, in parting from you now,

This much let me avow –
You are not wrong, who deem
That my days have been a dream;
Yet if Hope has flown away
In a night, or in a day,
In a vision, or in none,
Is it therefore the less gone?
All that we see or seem
Is but a dream within a dream.

— Edgar Allan Poe

SEVEN

A week passes quickly when one is busy and engrossed in tasks. Maddie still looked up from her desk every once and awhile just to check if Carson had showed up. It was Thursday morning when Harry telephoned. There was a dullness to his voice so she anticipated there was no news. He confirmed that this was developing into a true puzzler. No records were uncovered that might point to the whereabouts of Carson. The Town Police could not find anything either, reaffirming what she had found out earlier from them. Harry had even checked the county hospital to no avail. He ended the conversation with the assurance he would keep on checking. He then told her that his twin sons were anxious to meet her and would be over at some time in the afternoon. They would be giving her the copy of *Network of Death* that he had promised to lend to her. He further added that since they had a mystery of their own she should enjoy this one knowing it was pure fiction.

Maddie did not require further detective skills to conclude who the two students she saw through the glass door waiting outside of her office were. John and Michael Inman were identical twins, and the only way that she was sure she was not seeing double was that they were not dressed alike. They had slight builds but were as tall as their father.

When she finished assisting the student she was with, she motioned them in. After introductions, the twins sat in the two chairs in front of the desk. "I hope," she began cheerfully, "You two are not strangers to the Library."

Both shook their heads in near unison. Michael spoke first. "No, indeed. We study here often and dad encourages us to take advantage of this great place as much as we can."

"And, we do," John added.

"What are you both majoring in?"

"Political Science," John blurted out.

"Since Blantyre has a law school," Michael chimed in, "And since we get free tuition because of Dad's job, we'll go on to become lawyers."

Maddie smiled. "Makes sense to me. I don't have anything to do with the law books collections, but I do know that the holdings are extensive and that there is a separate law library reading room."

Michael looked at John before he spoke. He handed her the copy of Network of Death. "Here's the book Dad wanted to lend to you. Looks like you will be seeing plenty of us over the next four years."

Maddie laughed. "Maybe I'll be able to tell you apart by then."

After the twins left, Maddie was submerged in the work her training was geared for. Hoping soon to compile records, then there might be more spare time to further explore the holdings of the institution for her own pleasure. Once involved in the world of books there are no limits to the desire to find and know more.

On Friday, the letter she had sent to Mary Farrell was returned marked *Addressee Unknown*. Maddie telephoned Harry to report on it. His response was as she expected. He was not surprised and opined that even in the computer age people can disappear if they want or need to.

At Marie's place on Saturday evening Maddie reported on the returned letter and what Harry said. Marie felt that there was no certainty that Mary Farrell even existed. Then, she gushed with a thought. *Addressee Unknown* might be a good title for the book she was hoping to write. She joked that if anyone asked her if she had started with the writing she could in good conscience at least respond that she had a title.

They spent their usual pleasant time together. Marie was enthusiastic about how her classes were going. She took special delight in how eager most of the students were to learn and to write. Perhaps the overall disappointment she had cast on young people was not as deeply entrenched as she had thought. There was one young woman in particular, Honore Duvall, who captured her special attention. The student had a dynamic personality accompanied by a probing mind. It did not hurt either that she was French.

"Maybe we should form a French connection," Maddie offered.

"It does prompt a special bond, doesn't it?"

"There certainly are many French influences in our surroundings."

"Such as?"

"French wine, French bread, French fries, and French kisses, just to name some."

"I think you may confuse names with influences, but who am I to disagree. What we really need are French men."

"That would help but I am not fussy in that department."

"Are the twins possible romantic candidates?"

Maddie hesitated as she had not really thought of them in that regard. "In a way I suppose, but they are so young."

"You forget that you are young."

"True, yet I feel a certain maturity in a man is best for me."

"Why?"

"Stability, I suppose."

"There is enough of life ahead of you to cramp it with foolish restrictions. My advice to you is to live life to the fullest wherever, whenever, and however you can."

"Is that going to be Chapter One or the last chapter in your book?"

"It will be the overall theme. If you will do it I will cite you as an example."

"I'll take it under advisement." Maddie chuckled. "I will keep all of my options open. One way or another, I have always done that."

"Good."

"Yet, twins may be too much for me, excuse the pun."

"Just because there are two of them does not mean that you have to fall for both."

"They are both the same."

"As you get to know them, differences will emerge. And, whichever one you discard you can give to me."

Maddie laughed loudly. "They're not French."

It was Marie's turn to laugh. "There is a weakness in every theory, isn't there?"

> *Ah, when to the heart of man*
> *Was it ever less than a treason*
> *To go with the drift of things,*
> *To yield with a grace to reason,*
> *And bow and accept the end*
> *Of a love or a season?*

— Robert Frost

EIGHT

It was Tuesday afternoon when Harry telephoned. "I have news for you. Are you sitting down?"

That question presupposed that the news forthcoming was not good. "I'm sitting. You have my full attention."

"Carson Farrell was killed riding a motorcycle."

Maddie gasped. "Oh, my!"

"That's not all."

"I'm not sure I want to know more."

"He was killed in a small town in Georgia."

"Don't be dramatic and don't spare me the details."

"It's the details that are interesting. It was more than a year ago."

Maddie gasped again. "Then who or what is going on?"

"That's the twenty thousand dollar question. Someone decided to impersonate him. There is now a new mystery here."

"I never would have guessed this kind of development. Where do we go from here?"

"There has been a fraud committed against the University. The exact nature is uncertain, particularly since it was for such a brief time. I am not even sure any harm can be established. As far as I am concerned if this fellow does not reappear the case is closed as far as the University needs to be involved. All of the records here at the school will now show that Carson is deceased."

"I don't think it is the end for me. Call it a basic curiosity, but there has to be, at the least, a compelling story here. What would make anyone want to take the place of a dead student at a college, especially so determined to write a thesis? Also, what has happened to the impersonator? Has he been the victim of some criminal act?"

"Anything is possible, and I am of the opinion we will never know. Unless there has been some foul play that has taken place here on campus my hands are tied."

"Is there anything I can look into on an individual level?"

"I don't know what that might be. The best thing would be if he shows up and offers some sort of explanation. Other than that, try to put it behind you as just some sort of strange human behavior. People can do all kinds of outlandish acts, and I am not sure that they know themselves what they are doing and why. Life is too short to address the unknowns and the unknowables. If I hear anything further, I'll let you know."

"Thanks, Harry. You should be a professor here."

"Police tactics?"

"No. Life 101."

When Maddie telephoned Marie that evening with the unusual developments, she was equally surprised by it all. "That would have been the last thing I would have guessed."

"Me, too. I doubt I will sleep tonight. I am too keyed up, and imagine all sorts of possibilities that make me shiver. I will be looking out for Carson, or whoever he is, every day I am sure. I don't suppose I'll calm down until I know what happened, not to mention the whys."

"Harry gave you good advice. You have a job to do and you need to make a life of your own. You may never know what happened or why. You need to rise above it and concentrate on yourself and your new life here. Do you want me to come over and keep you company?"

"You're a dear, but you must have much to do at your end. I'll take a walk and then have a glass of wine. Then I'll lose myself in the book Harry lent me."

"Sounds like just what the doctor would order. Be at peace, mademoiselle."

The walk and wine did help. The book, however, did not. The

story had so many twists and turns that it further stimulated her mind. She could not help but finish it before she took a shower and got into bed. How some people can plan a mystery story and then set it to writing is a real gift. The similarities and contrasts to the real mystery she was faced with were apparent. With the book, she was baffled until she reached the end, and even that ending left many questions which required a sequel. The so-called Carson mystery might never have any kind of ending.

> *Heart, are you great enough*
> *   For a love that never tires?*
> *O heart, are you great enough for love?*
> *   I have heard of thorns and briers.*
> *Over the thorns and briers,*
> *   Over the meadows and stiles,*
> *Over the world to the end of it*
> *   Flash for a million miles.*

> — Alfred Lord Tennyson

NINE

There were no calming or reflective poet's dreams to offset the bouts of restlessness during the night. A good night's sleep was also disturbed by a hard rain with ice pellets lashing against the windows. Maddie arose early and she stared out of the window at increasing daylight accentuating the forceful rain. She sipped on her second cup of coffee and nibbled on an English muffin with orange marmalade. A brief thought of why it was an English muffin instead of a French muffin gave way to dismal projections of a poorly clothed youth shivering in the wet and cold. Being the romantic and infused with an Ethical Culture upbringing, it was difficult to imagine such a youth being at the mercy of some evil act. She debated whether to tell her parents about it all since they were mature and level-headed and long experienced journalists who might well have a different and rational slant on the turn of events. Yet, she knew they would worry, especially being thousands of miles away. As the product of a vast reader of literature, even at the most inopportune moment some phrase that had stuck in her mind would emerge. Thinking about her parents worrying, a quote by the American author Leo Buscaglia came to her head. *Worry never robs tomorrow of its sorrow, it only saps today of its joy.*

Wearing a wool pants suit, boots, a hat, and a raincoat over a heavy jacket, she set out for the Library early. There was still some ice mixed in with the rain and she walked gingerly along the slippery walkways. Somehow, there was something comforting about an example of Nature's fury. No one else was around and the sound of the precipitation on the umbrella kept her company while walking carefully was a distraction.

The first thing Maddie did at the office was to make some coffee. She imagined asking Carson, or whatever his name was, if he wanted a cup. Then she did a computer search on the motorcycle accident and obituaries. Nothing was found, and that was puzzling. She forced herself to let it go as she had some engrossing and challenging work to do. A better night's rest would have helped, although she knew her motivation and intelligence would see her through it.

She was planning to take *Network of Death* back to Harry on her lunch break, but it was still pouring so she decided she would do it on her way home. The rain had stopped by then. Harry was not there. Another officer was at the desk, a young man intent on a bunch of papers spread out before him. He looked up after she knocked and entered the room. "Greetings," he said in a low voice. He stood up and as she approached him she could see that the name badge on his police shirt read *Alexander.* He was short, not much taller than Maddie. His nose was too large for his face and had a definite slant to the left. His ears were also disproportionately large for the face. Although far from what one might describe as handsome, the face was pleasant and he had a warm smile which seemed to need little prompting to appear. He was wearing jeans, and Maddie surmised that the whole force probably only wore complete uniforms for ceremonial occasions.

"I'm looking for Harry," she said with a smile of her own.

"Harry works the day shift. I am the officer on duty from four to midnight, officer Alexander. Can I help you with something?"

She stood before the desk and noticed that the papers were a course study. "Alexander is your first or last name?"

"Last. My first name is William but I only respond to Will."

"I am Maddie Ponte, French as you have probably already figured out. I work in the Collections Department at the Library."

"Ah, I now match a face with a name. I read Harry's report. We don't have much going on here so every report is fully digested by all of us."

"And what do you make of it?"

"Have a seat if you have a moment." After she sat in the chair before the desk he sat and then continued. "My guess is that this fellow, for whatever personal reason he may have had, wanted to take the real Carson's place. He then got cold feet and either realized he probably would not get away with it or that it was not worth getting away with. After all, the rigors of college study, especially this college, is no walk in the park. I should know, I'm a junior and the past two years have been a major academic struggle. The faculty is demanding and the student body eager and bright. There is competition at every level."

"Maybe working full time gives you great pressure."

He chuckled. "I wish I could use that as an excuse. Actually, because there is little activity here I have ample time to study. The job is a means to an end. The pay is meager but I get free tuition, a free single room in a dorm, and an annual free cafeteria meal ticket. The single room is required because I am on call 24/7 just in case of a case and have contact equipment in the room and on me at all times. The police cruiser I use I park in the front of the dorms as it may have some deterrent effect although that is probably not necessary here."

She was intent on studying his face. "You know, you look familiar to me. Have we met before?"

"I was thinking the same thing about you. We probably passed each other in the cafeteria or on campus. As a police officer I try to be as observant about everything, and that includes people. Further, it is easy to remember a pretty face that speaks with a delightful French accent."

"Besides a police officer you are a corn ball. Are you majoring in charm?"

"Forensic Science."

They chatted for a few minutes attempting to narrow down the possibility they had met before. Eventually, much to their surprise, they discovered they had both been at the Ethical Culture School at the same time although Will had been two years ahead of her. His story was a sad one. In his senior high school year his father had pancreatic cancer and died before the graduation. The funds that had been saved for his college education went towards medical and related bills even with insurance. Will did not know at that time what he wanted to study. He joined the New York Police Department, was fully trained and then assigned to a detective's unit. He gradually became intrigued with forensic investigations. After four years this opportunity at Blantyre opened up and it was too attractive to pass up.

On Maddie's side there was not as much to relate. When she brought the tale up to the moment she wanted to start back home and left the book for Harry with a note attached to it.

They shook hands. Will mentioned that he did not have much spare time outside of his duties which involved the Campus Police four to twelve shift six days a week. On Wednesday's the office was not manned, but they all had the communication devices at hand. The third officer, Nigel Burnside, handled the midnight to eight shift. Maddie was not sure Will was telling her all of this because he did not want to see her again or could not see her. It made little difference. Despite the common background, she did not feel any initial attraction to him although she never turned her back on the possibility of friendships.

Wine comes in at the mouth
And love comes in at the eye;
That's all we shall know for truth
Before we grow old and die.
I lift the glass to my mouth,
I look at you, and I sigh.

— William Butler Yeats

TEN

Marie came to Maddie's for dinner on Saturday night. Furthering the custom she had in hand a bottle of French wine. Maddie made veal cutlets with a side of fresh spinach. While they were eating, Maddie related the meeting with Will. Marie's reaction was as anticipated. "Another bird on the wire! Twins and now a cop, while I have nobody. Not fair, I say."

"You sure like having fun with me, don't you?"

"You should have kept it a secret about being a romantic. Now you are fair game."

"I don't mind really, but I don't think teasing me about it will make it so. I don't have that kind of interest in any of them."

"So you say. Things have a way of changing. The down side will be that the field will get so crowded that you may not recognize the real one when he comes along."

"Not a chance!"

After the dessert, a store bought blueberry tart, they sat in the living room finishing the wine. Maddie showed Marie a more recent one of her poems. Marie read it through carefully twice just as she did with the earlier poem. "You have a charming style and it is apparent the more you create the smoother the tones and ideas. Added to your talent is plenty of heart. I can't encourage you enough to keep on writing."

"Your very kind words help, but I do not intend to abandon an activity that is a part of me."

"Now that that is settled, are you abandoning the quest to find the mystery man?"

"There is nothing more I can do. I just hope he shows up so I can get some rest."

"And if he doesn't?"

"I'll have no choice but to live with a nagging unknown."

"I bet the undercurrent of your poetry will be different."

"How so?"

"Less romantic and with a twinge of melancholy."

"Perhaps. I hope not. While life can be cruel, I will always believe it is capable of bringing about beautiful things."

"Compassion for the large and small."

"Something like that."

"Loose ends can be unnerving."

"So I now know."

They were quiet for a few minutes. Silence between friends can be its own form of communicating. There is no such thing as an awkward silence because there are no expectancies and no judgment. Comfort is derived just in the company and the knowing of interest and concern. Maddie cherished all of her friends and she was so glad she kept in touch with them. It was akin to a support group. That network would help in keeping perspective on the vicissitudes of life. Of course, the best situation is having a friend at your side as Marie was. The problem with the feeling she had that another human being was calling out for help was that she might have been able to do something about it if she had recognized it earlier. Due to her tender years and strong beliefs, all incidents have an impact on her thoughts and behavior. They undoubtedly affect her poetry. Marie called that verse growth and maturity. Maddie only hoped it would not crimp her spirit and outlook.

Marie then elaborated on her favorite student, Honore Duvall. The young woman had a deep literary talent, and she brightened the class with quips and pointed comments. Marie saw in her the youngster she had wished she had been as well as the prime example for the message she wanted to convey in her forthcoming book. She was anxious for Maddie to meet her so she had suggested to Honore to visit her at the Library. The way Marie saw it, if two peas should be in the same pod, she would arrange for a pod happening. That would make her a podster. Inventing new words can be rewarding.

After Marie left, Maddie was not sleepy although she should have been. The stimulating conversation with Marie and the nagging unknown over the lost soul infused Maddie with a form of restlessness that required poetry writing to quiet.

Life has so many facets you cannot master them all,
And as short as life can be it is highly unlikely
you can be exposed to every one;
So, the key is how to manage each venture, large or small,
Yet even that illusive key may only be found by some.

Even if there is doubt as to what it is or how to proceed,
It is worth the exploration, the urge to taste;
Otherwise, the desire to experience what it is like to succeed
Will end up in the negative category of a waste.

Perhaps the real secret is not what life might be,
Rather the courage to try what is not fully understood;
To proclaim you have tried it even without mastery,
To have done as much as you could.

Maddie took a shower and then sat by the window staring out into the night until her hair dried. Carson, or whatever his name was, is out there somewhere. She could only hope that he would find a light at the end of his dark tunnel.

And what delights can equal those
That stir the spirit's inner deeps,
When one that loves, but knows not, reaps
A truth from one that loves and knows?

— Alfred Lord Tennyson

ELEVEN

At times, answers come either too soon or in forms we are not prepared for. Early Monday morning Harry telephoned. "You won't want to hear this, but there is no way to say it except as it is. Last night a body was discovered in the river on the other side of town." Maddie moaned loudly. "It is, rather it was, a young male with a beard. The body was naked so there was no identification. There were no marks on the body either. It has been taken to the morgue which is behind the County Hospital. Since you may be the only person who can tell if it is this Carson fellow, would you mind going there and taking a look?"

Maddie attempted to keep her composure and be professional. The last thing she would want to do would be to look at a dead body. Yet, it might present a closure of sorts. "I suppose so. I have no car, no way of getting there."

"I'm on duty and can't leave the office. If you can get away at lunch time I'll have Will drive you over there. He mentioned he met you."

"Please tell Will I'll be in front of the Library at twelve."

"Right. Have you ever seen a dead body before?"

"No."

"It's not pleasant, but you'll get through it. Plus, it's the way to maybe get some answers."

"That's why I will do it. If I get nightmares from it, I will hold you responsible."

"I have broad shoulders, and," he paused for a moment and

Maddie thought there was something else he was going to say, "We all have nightmares of one kind or another."

Will was waiting in the police cruiser as she descended the steps from the Library. They exchanged greetings and he motioned for her to get in the front seat.

They made light conversation on the fifteen minute trip. It was obvious he was trying to put her at ease, and she appreciated that and told him so. She liked his response. "Many people don't take the little effort that it may take to ease a trying situation or to lessen an unhappy moment. That's one of the problems in this ever-increasing cold society."

She did not respond immediately. "Then it is up to each of us to do something about it."

"Would be nice."

"It certainly would."

The morgue was a small nondescript building nearly rundown. Will had been told it had been a barber shop in the early days. Even though small it was adequate for the amount of suspicious or unknown dead bodies. For the one morgue there were more than a dozen funeral parlors spread around the county.

They entered the old and dark building, and Maddie felt a chill spread up her spine. This was the last place she would ever want to be at. An elderly man was sitting at a desk in an outer room. The opening of the door probably awoke him from a nap. He led them to the back room, where there was a wall high refrigerated unit with rows of large drawers. He pulled out one of the drawers on which there was a body completely covered by a while sheet.

The man pulled the sheet down from the body's face. Maddie knew immediately that it was not Carson but it was a ghastly sight nonetheless. She could not even tell if it was a young face though Harry had said the man was young. The skin was ashen, the lips blue, and the beard was stiff and matted. Looking at death, Maddie resolved to live her life to the fullest. Whatever the cause or reason for the death before her, she would bask in the fruits of her existence.

She shook her head towards Will and quickly turned away. Will put his arm around her shoulder and supported her on the way back to the car. She could not stop shaking. He stopped at the gas station at the intersection and bought her a hot coffee. She sipped it as they drove. "Thank you for understanding," her voice was cracking as well.

"There is nothing to worry about. It is gruesome even for those hardened to such an event. To make things worse he was probably in the water for a long time."

"What do you think happened to him?"

"There are no visible marks on the body which usually indicates foul play. Undoubtedly, an autopsy will be done. My guess is that it is a suicide. At some point there may be a suicide note which will reveal much. If there is no note they'll try to piece the story together from his belongings and the content of his computer."

"How will he ever be identified?"

"There should be a missing person's report forthcoming. They will also run his fingerprints."

"Why was he naked?"

"Beats me, but I guess it is a symbolic thing that he was shedding society before he shed his life. To my way of thinking suicide is never an answer. It is so final. There just has to be other solutions. Of course, to him there probably seemed to be no other solutions or he believed he had tried everything else to no avail. I admire those persons who work in the suicide prevention field. Any success must be so rewarding."

Draining the last of the coffee, Maddie sighed. "I feel as if I have aged a year in this one day. I could cry for him."

"Me, too. That's another aspect, it is cruel for those loved ones left behind."

Will dropped her at the Library steps. He tried to inject a humorous note, but as it came out he realized he was serious about it. "If I had the time, I'd ask you for a date."

She half smiled. The response she gave was the one she had prepared to give if one of the twins had proposed such a happening. "I'm considered a faculty member for socialization purposes and there is a prohibition on faculty members dating students. Technically, you are a student."

He grinned. "Not when I am in uniform."

Were you the earth, dear Love, and I the skies,
My love should shine on you like to the sun,
And look upon you with ten thousand eyes
Till heaven wax'd blind, and till the world were done.

Whereso'er I am, below, or else above you,
Whereso'er you are, my heart shall truly love you.

— Joshua Sylvester

TWELVE

Maddie had telephoned Marie about the body, although they did not really discuss it until Maddie arrived for dinner Saturday night. Both were looking forward to the wine as much as the feast that Marie had prepared.

"So," Marie blurted out, "Have you heard any more about the corpse?"

"Harry called me yesterday just to tell me there was no news yet. There has been no local missing person report so there is speculation that he may have traveled some distance to get here. They're expanding the collection of reports from the rest of the state as well as the adjoining states. The autopsy indicates that the cause of death was hypothermia and the lungs were filled with water which means he was alive when he jumped in. It doesn't totally rule out murder, but a suicide is still the prevailing theory."

"I guess it proves there are dark shadows in many places."

Maddie was pensive. "It can be frightening to think what lies in such places."

"As you know, I was in such place at one time. It is more than scary. You can crave the light but there is none to be found."

"Morbid thoughts, for sure. Let's turn to lighter matters."

"At least we know there are no dark places here."

"Friendship carries its own bright light."

"Warm, too, to ward off the cold."

"Funny you should say that. The colder it gets the more I think about Carson shivering somewhere."

"You have one large heart, Frenchie."

"I'm starting to think that may not always be a good thing."

"It's not, but it is you. You couldn't change it even if you wanted to."

"All things considered, there is much you may have to put in your book. It may wind up to be a heavy tome in more ways than one."

Marie glanced away almost as if there was a third person there that she wanted to include in the conversation. "And, so I shall." A brief hesitation and she made an effort to change the subject. "Who is your favorite poet?

"You."

Marie laughed. "You get an A for that. Of the masters, who do you keep coming back to?"

"Interesting you should put it that way. I do not have a particular favorite although I am often drawn to William Wordsworth. His poetry can be complex and it can contain so many intermingling deep thoughts begging to be reread and inspiring much conjecture. There are thoughts and ideas that inspire the reader to think well beyond the verses. Of the classic style, who do you feel closest to?"

"It would have to be Elizabeth Barrett Browning. When I got married, before I discovered that he was not worthy of me or the marriage, I memorized one of her poems and recited it at the wedding. It is committed to my memory as a lasting tribute to her talent, I suppose, and when I was still a romantic and before that got stomped in the dirt."

How do I love thee? Let me count the ways.
I love thee to the depth and breadth and height
My soul can reach, when feeling out of sight
For the ends of Being and ideal Grace.
I love thee to the level of everyday's
Most quiet need, by sun and candle-light.
I love thee freely, as men strive for Right;
I love thee purely, as they turn from Praise.

I love thee with the passion put to use
In my old griefs, and with my childhood's faith.
I love thee with a love I seemed to lose
With my lost saints, – I love thee with the breath,
Smiles, tears, of all my life!   And, if God choose,
I shall but love thee better after death.

"Yes, that is beautiful."

"Women make history."

"Women should have controlled history.   There would have been far fewer wars."

"Awomen!"

Thanks to the human heart by which we live,
Thanks to the tenderness, its joys and fears,
To me the meanest flower that blows can give
Thoughts that do often lie too deep for tears.

— William Wordsworth

THIRTEEN

On Sunday, Maddie caught up with talking to her parents and answering emails and letters from friends. She mentioned Will not as a romantic interest but just for the coincidence of meeting another Ethical Culture School graduate. Her parents were quite happy to be ensconced in France, and they were looking forward to Maddie's visit over Christmas. There had been two wedding invitations in the mail. Her friends were of marrying age, so there would be some memorable moments ahead. Because of time and distance constraints, she doubted she would be able to attend the ceremonies, although she would send a hefty check to assist the couples on their travel along life's highway. There was no envy. The dream of her romantic union was unshaken and unshakeable.

Mid-morning on Monday a woman knocked on her office door. Maddie could see through the glass that it was a petite and pretty young woman with long red hair. In fact, the woman was nearly a mirror reflection of herself even with her own black hair. "Ms. Ponte?," the young woman inquired.

"In the flesh. Do you need some reference assistance?"

"Perpetually," the woman groaned. "But, I just stopped by to meet you. I am Honore Duvall."

"Come in. I was told you might show up."

The young woman sat in the chair by the desk and crossed a shapely leg encased in a black leotard beneath a short plaid skirt. "Nice office."

Maddie smiled. "It is really a work shop. Do you like libraries?"

"Books have been my good friends most of my life. I grew up in a small town in Connecticut. The town was even too small for a library, but my father was a teacher and my parents were strong readers. They had an extensive collection of books, so it almost felt like I lived in a library. I didn't read all of them but I like to brag I made a good dent in them."

"I discovered libraries early on and I am at home here. I shudder each time I think of how much wisdom surrounds me and all I have to do is to reach out for it."

"I can appreciate that."

"What are you majoring in?"

"I am just a freshman, but I am leaning towards English."

"Do you want to be a teacher like your father?"

"Maybe, although I am not sure. Being a writer, a poet, or just a know-it-all appeals to me. I have an insatiable intellectual appetite."

"That's a good foundation for many edifices. Enjoy the trip. You have time to fix on a destination."

"I plan to do just that. Meanwhile, I would like to know I have made a new friend in high places."

"I'm just a lowly collections librarian, but I do know the way in the world of research. If I can guide you, just stop by."

"Very nice of you. One can always use some directions on the road to know-it-all."

Maddie chuckled. "And there are many sights to enjoy along the way. Don't rush the traveling."

"I won't. I like to think I recognize opportunity when I come across it."

Maddie was not quite sure what she she meant by that, although she would soon find out. "Good for you. Good luck."

"Thanks." Honore rose and spoke in a hushed voice as she put her hand over Maddie's fingers. "I am very attracted to you. Can we meet privately?"

Maddie should have been shocked, but growing up in New York City she had seen much and heard about even more. At school she had never been approached directly, although she had seen signs of girls in affectionate close situations. She offered what now seemed to be a standard response. "I am considered a faculty member and there is a strict prohibition about socialization with a student."

Honore responded in a low whisper. "No one else will ever know."

Maddie attempted to sound stern. "That's not the point. I am a city girl and certainly not out of touch with what is going on in the world. Yet, I believe that love is only between a man and a woman. It is not a religious belief as I am not religious. It is a firm outlook that I have developed for myself, a faith in one kind of relationship that is significant for me and that will be truly meaningful. It is my bedrock."

"No man can love you like another woman. No man can kiss you as gently as another woman. The advice you just gave me holds true for you. On the trip enjoy the sights, and partake in all of the feelings and sensations."

"You need to respect the lifestyle other people choose for themselves. I don't sit in judgment of the choices others make. If you want us to be friends you will have to accept that."

Honore removed her hand. "I can live with that even though I wish it otherwise. You may change your mind. It has been known to happen."

Honore rushed out the door and Maddie was not sure if she heard her response. "Not a chance."

When Maddie telephoned Marie that evening to tell her that Honore came for a visit and that she was a lesbian, Marie replied, "She has not tried to hit on me. I suppose she realizes I have the power to flunk her. As it is, I am not really surprised and such behavior will be in the book. Girls, especially when in college and away from the restrictions of the home experiment in all sorts of relationships. I suppose you could argue that it is beneficial to get certain things out of their system rather than brood about it all of their lives. Most will settle down in the conventional main stream. Since you have apparently made a better connection with her than I have, maybe you can talk to her more about it all. A realistic outlook, offsetting obscure influences can work wonders."

"I'm no expert in these things, and I have enough problems in my own life so I certainly am not going to tell someone else what they should or should not do."

"You know the value of just listening, and most young people cry for a person to listen. You do not abandon you.   You just don't abandon them."

"I do not turn my back on one I can help."

"Good. That's the French way."

While she who could for love dispense
With all its glittering accidents,
And trust her heart alone,
Finds love and gold her own.

What wealth can buy or art can build
Awaits her; but her cup is filled
Even now unto the brim;
Her world is love and him!

— John Greenleaf Whittier

FOURTEEN

On Wednesday Will showed up just before noon with a coffee and pastry for her. "It's sort of my day off. I know from our morgue trip you like coffee black and the store told me this was a French pastry, although I wouldn't know a French pastry if I fell over it. I thought you might like some unofficial police attention."

Maddie smiled. "Very thoughtful and I thank you. I usually don't eat lunch. I have a hearty breakfast and a good dinner. I might have a yogurt or a piece of fruit. I need to stay slim to get through the stacks. This is a special treat, so I'll make an exception today. Please sit down and I'll give you half of the pastry."

He sat in the side chair and she cut the pastry in half with a fork she had by the coffee pot. "Would you like me to make some coffee for you to go with the pastry?"

"No, thanks. I've already had my limit for today. I am due at a class and have to rush off. I just don't want you to forget me."

"I do not forget kindnesses."

He grinned. "By the way, still nothing on the corpse."

"I figured that since Harry hadn't called."

He stood up and as he turned to leave he said sheepishly, "Keep your pretty nose in the books."

"I'm certainly going to keep it out of other people's business." Little did she know at that moment that those words would come back to haunt her.

She worked a little later than usual, and by the time she departed from the Library towards home the walkway was nearly deserted. It had turned very cold and there were snow flurries accentuated in the lights from the lamp posts along the walkway. Darkness often added a sharper bite to the cold. She tightened the coat around her and pulled the wool cap down over her ears.

Once inside her home, she had just taken off the coat and hung it in the closet when there was a knock at the door. She looked through the peephole, gasped loudly and closed her eyes for an instant. It was Carson.

Being a city girl and highly attuned to danger and conditioned to exercise precaution at every turn, normally she would have spoken through the closed locked door. Whether it was a sense of relief, exasperation, or just plain old curiosity, she flung open the door. Carson was standing there shivering wearing the same thin frayed sweatshirt.

She grabbed him by the arm and pulled him inside, closing the door behind him. "You are the last person I ever expected to see."

His voice was unsteady. "Sorry to bother you, ma'am. I was waiting outside of the Library and followed you here. You are the only person who has shown any concern, and I owe you an explanation."

She sensed she was in no danger. Her voice softened. "Sit at the table. You must be frozen. I'll get you some hot soup."

He sat, and she opened up a can of soup, poured it into a bowl and started the microwave. She could not help but notice that his eyes were half closed. Besides being cold he must be exhausted. He managed to stutter, "I waited for you for over an hour."

"You should have come inside."

After a brief hesitation, he muttered, "I did not want to be seen."

She did not like the sound of that. "It will be just a minute for the soup to be hot and then you can tell me everything."

He did not say anything but watched her intently. She sat across from him as she placed the bowl of soup before him. He devoured the soup. When finished, he sat back and looked directly into the soft dark eyes. "This will certainly sound foolish to you, and maybe it is. My real name is Nate Farrell. Carson Farrell was my brother. He died in a terrible motorcycle accident more than a year ago. He was a year older than me although we were very, very close. He was the smart one, much smarter than I am. He was valedictorian in high school, had an academic scholarship to college and then the full scholarship here. I was lucky to have gotten through high school. I was good with my hands and became an auto mechanic. I have been able to work on the old car I have now and keep it going. Carson shared many of the things he learned with me, and I loved him that much more that he did not consider me inferior. He was a deep thinker and told me all the details of the hopes he had for achievements in life. He talked continuously about the topic for his thesis and was so excited about undertaking it. I admired him and loved him. Before his accident our mother was in a hospice and dying slowly. I just knew if she found out about his terrible death it would have killed her on the spot. So, I was able to stifle any news report about the accident and not have an obituary printed about him." He stopped speaking and rubbed his eyes as if that magically would make the weariness and sadness all go away. "After our mother died, I had a crazy idea. Since no one officially knew of Carson's death, I would take his place here and do the thesis. I would be fulfilling his dream. I could not think of a better tribute to him. However, once I got here and started on it I realized I was kidding myself. I do not have the intelligence or even the fortitude to really get into it. I am staying at a rundown motel in the next town over and working part time as a mechanic to pay for the motel. That day you gave me the coffee I became sick and went back to the motel. For two weeks I laid there punishing myself for such a cockeyed plan that I didn't stand a chance to carry out. It is as if I died with Carson."

He was silent with his eyes cast down to the table. Maddie felt a great compassion for his plight. "You are being too hard on yourself. You wanted to do something good and you tried to do it. That is more than many would do in a similar situation. That alone is a tribute to your brother."

"Again, ma'am, you are far too kind."

"What are you going to do?"

Nate stared deep into those caring dark eyes. "The only thing I can do. I parked behind the Library. I have packed the few things I have and I'll go back to Georgia and try to get my old job back.

Somehow, I'll manage to keep Carson's memory alive."

Maddie threw all caution to the wind. "Not tonight you are not going. You are exhausted and half-frozen. You can sleep on the sofa and start out in the morning. She brought out some sheets, a pillow, and two blankets. She made up the sofa for him and then went to the bedroom. She had the feeling there was nothing to fear from Nate, and she closed the door but did not lock it. She had not eaten and was not hungry. Even though she felt sorry for Nate she felt at ease. After reading for awhile she fell into a better sleep than she had for awhile.

The alarm went off at seven. She put on a robe over the sweatsuit she wore to bed and went to the kitchen. Nate was already gone. The sheets and blankets were neatly folded on the sofa. There was no note. Just as with the initial coffee, as well as the soup the night before, there was no thank you for her involvement. Yet, in a way Maddie felt his gratitude, and she smiled. She wished him well wherever he went in this life. She also knew that she would never hear from him again, but she was content with that. There was the relief that nothing bad had happened to him, and she had helped in some way.

Maddie telephone Marie right away. "Sorry, if I awoke you."

"I am up. Is something wrong?"

"I had a visit from Carson's ghost last night."

"What!"

Maddie conveyed the entire story, ending with, "Nate is on his way back to Georgia."

Marie whistled. "Are you sure you are not an angel dressed as a librarian?"

"For my book of living, one chapter is complete."

A heart as soft, a heart as kind,
  A heart as sound and free
As in the whole world thou canst find,
  That heart I'll give to thee.

Bid that heart stay, and it will stay,
*   To honour thy decree:*
Or bid it languish quite away,
*   And't shall do so for thee.*

Bid me to weep, and I will weep
*   While I have eyes to see:*
And having none, yet I will keep
*   A heart to weep for thee.*

Bid me despair, and I'll despair,
*   Under that cypress tree:*
Or bid me die, and I will dare
*   E'en Death, to die for thee.*

Thou art my life, my love, my heart,
*   The very eyes of me,*
And hast command of every part,
*   To live and die for thee.*

— Robert Herrick

BOOK TWO

Needs and Deeds

Our slender life runs rippling by, and glides
   Into the silent hollow of the past;
      What is there that abides
   To make the next age better for the last?
      Is earth too poor to give us
Something to live for here that shall outlive us?
      Some more substantial boon
Than such as flows and ebbs with Fortune's fickle moon?
      The little that we see
      From doubt is never free;
      The little that we do
         Is but half-nobly free;
   With our laborious hiving
What men call treasure, and the gods call dross,
   Life seems a jest of Fate's contriving,
   Only secure in every one's conniving.
A long account of nothings paid with loss,
Were we poor puppets, jerked by unseen wires,
   After our little hour of strut and rave,
With all our pasteboard passions and desires,
Loves, hates, ambitions, and immortal fires,
   Are tossed pell-mell together in the grave.
   But stay! no age was e'er degenerate,
   Unless men held it at too cheap a rate,
   For in our likeness still we shape our fate.
    Ah, there is something here
   Unfathomed by the cynic's sneer,

Daniel Hill Zafren

Something that gives our feeble light
  A high immunity from Night,
  Something that leaps life's narrow bars
To claim its birthright with the hosts of heaven;
  A seed of sunshine that can leaven
  Our earthly dullness with the beams of stars,
    And glorify our clay
With light from fountains elder than the Day;
  A conscience more divine than we,
  A gladness fed with secret tears,
  A vexing, forward-reaching sense
  Of some more noble permanence;
    A light across the sea,
  Which haunts the soul and will not let it be,
Still beaconing from the heights of undegenerate years.

— James Russell Lowell

FIFTEEN

The two weeks over Christmas break in Paris was just what Maddie needed. She had been exhausted from the job and the soothing and relaxing time with her parents fixed her right up. Despite the uneasy feeling in the city from recent terrorist incidents, she took long walks along the promenades and avenues and frequented many of the cafes for ethnic tidbits. Each time she had wine she thought of Marie, and in a way felt sorry leaving her for the holiday because Marie was at Blantyre by herself. Her parents were deceased and she had distanced herself from them anyway. There were no other relatives or close friends she could spend the holiday with. At least Maddie knew that once her parents were not around, she had close friends she could visit and share special times with.

She also felt sorry for Will. He was still on duty through the holiday break as the college was officially open. Some of the dorms remained occupied with students who could not travel. University property had to be protected. The cafeteria was closed so he had to go to town to eat. At least his mother came to visit for a few days. Maddie had developed a friendship with Will. On his day off, she would meet him at the cafeteria and would have a light lunch with him. She had him wear his uniform even though it was his day off so no one would think she was socializing with a student. Will had a good sense of humor, and just through conversation she learned about forensics. Maddie knew Will liked her and would be eager for a romantic involvement. She just did not have that same inclination towards him and was content to leave it as a friendship.

On the long flight back Maddie also thought about the body found in the river. It had not been identified. No one had reported the young man missing. It was sad to think that a person could die and nobody cared about it. A sharp pang in her heart revealed her innate compassion. She would probably never know what misery and torment the man had to endure that led to the taking of his own life. She wondered if he had reached out for help, and that too would be tragic if there was no one there to help him. Another lesson learned in her young life was that tragedy can happen anywhere, at any time, and to any person. Not that one can actually prepare for it, but the possibility should be recognized and such should bring added impetus to living each and every moment to the fullest.

Maddie had not thought more about Honore, mainly perhaps because the young woman had not stopped by to see her again. In a way she was relieved about not having to give any further explanations, but she suspected the situation was not totally resolved. Honore was a clever young lady and she might merely be using time to her advantage. Hopefully, she had found another love interest. In spite of Marie's suggestion, Maddie preferred not to get involved with any extended discussions in shaping other people's ideas or life styles. It took much of her effort and energy to focus on the ever challenging responsibilities of her job. She loved her work and she wanted to succeed in its entire undertaking.

At least she did not have to contend with any overtures from the twins. They had stopped by a few times for a brief visit, but neither one suggested any social contact outside of the Library. Perhaps Harry was conversant enough about the University's regulations to warn them about any advances. Perhaps they were merely intimidated by her position. Whatever, it was something she did not have to contend with, and Maddie surely appreciated that as something good. The good things are their own outcome.

Maddie tried to talk her out of it, but Marie insisted she come to Boston to pick Maddie up at the airport. She wailed that she had the time and did not want the younger woman to have to take a limo. Her prevailing argument was that it would serve as a good opportunity to catch up on things. Since Marie did not do much during the break,

Forever Old, Forever New

Maddie did most of the talking. Marie did have one big news item. She had started writing the book, and Maddie greeted the news with great enthusiasm as she wanted to be as encouraging as possible. She also gave Marie half of the wine that she was able to get through customs.

Back at her living quarters, the first thing she did was to Skype her parents to let them know she had arrived safely. There was then a bunch of mail and emails to catch up on. There was one more day before she had to report for work, and she would go to the food store to stock up as well as clean the house. After a long shower, some reading, the time difference caught up with her and she fell asleep.

She awoke early the next morning gleefully noting that it had snowed a few inches over night. It was enough to convert the landscape to a magical setting. The snow clung to each branch and bush and lay pristinely along the walkways and the extensive lawn areas. It was as if the world was at peace, and Maddie only wished that such a wonderful essence would actually come true. It all seemed to match her inner calmness. Sure, she had yet to find the love she craved for, but so many other wonderful things surrounded her. All persons would benefit by taking a moment to survey the positives in their lives, and no doubt it would produce the same kind of inner tranquility. While there could always be more, most people would realize that their lives were in fact full and rich in the sense that there are so many things to be grateful for. Maddie also believed that such an uplifted attitude aided in recognizing and appreciating the successes in meeting each day's accomplishments. Having a good attitude is a precursor to happiness.

We are not sure of sorrow,
  And joy was never sure;
To-day will die tomorrow
  Time stoops to no man's lure;
And love, grown faint and fretful
With lips but half regretful

Sighs, and with eyes forgetful
Weeps that no loves endure.

— Algernon Charles Swinburne

SIXTEEN

Back at her work area in the Library, Maddie was absorbed in sorting out the tasks she had to catch up on. Will stopped by to welcome her back, and she gave him the French chocolate bar she brought back for him. He claimed it could not possibly be as sweet as she was.

It was early afternoon when the predicted blizzard began. The University officials closed the school down an hour later. There were few students around by the time the Library was cleared out and locked up. Maddie hated to stop working but recognized that the safety of all was the prime concern. Since she had heard the forecast before she had left home, she was prepared for the trek back with heavy coat, scarf, hat, gloves, and boots. The snow was coming down so hard and fast and wind-driven that it was sideways and it was difficult to see and maintain her balance.

Something moved in the snow in the path before her. At first, she thought it was a squirrel trying to make progress in the snow back to its tree nest. She had to stoop down to finally see that it was actually a small dog shivering violently in the wet and cold. Even over the howling wind Maddie could hear the dog whimpering. At a loss of what else to do, she picked up the nearly weightless animal, unbuttoned her coat part way and slipped the dog inside.

When she was inside the house, she dried the dog well with a towel and cradled it in her arms under a blanket until she was sure it was warm. It was a chestnut color, evidently a short-haired breed, and it had no collar. Maddie had never had a pet and knew little about animals. Animals were not allowed in the building that the family had lived in. She folded the blanket into a bed and placed it on the floor in the kitchen. Spreading a copy of the college weekly newspaper nearby, there was no way to know if the dog was house broken. She could not even tell if it was a puppy or just a tiny adult canine.

Maddie telephoned Will asking him if he knew about any report of a missing dog. He was not aware of any and would check. He called back twenty minutes later to advise there was no report, and he had checked with the town police with a similar result. There was no veterinarian in town. The nearest one was in the next town over, just down from the morgue. Will gave her the number. She called but the office was closed due to the weather. Maddie then called Harry to see if he had any ideas. The only thing he could come up with besides the fact that the County Animal Shelter was even further away was that he was acquainted with a professor in the Law School, Sy Burnwell, who had mentioned to him on one occasion that he went to Veterinarian School for a year before he dropped out to become a lawyer instead. He mentioned that Burnwell also happened to be in Maddie's same housing complex. He looked up the telephone number and gave it to her.

The voice that greeted her call was deep and pleasant. After a brief description of her plight, he was informative and reassuring. He told her not to give the dog any food or water. Dogs should only have dog food and be in a completely calm state before drinking any water. Since he has a dog, he has dog food and some other items she might find useful until the storm passed and the owner could be located. When he learned that she lived close by, he offered to trudge through the snow to bring the items to her.

At the sound of the doorbell, she opened the door to be greeted by a snowman. He was totally snow covered. She ushered him in and helped him off with his coat. He removed his hat and boots. Maddie had just assumed he would be older, but he was young, much too young to fit a perception of a law professor. He was also strikingly handsome with a quick and easy smile. He handed her the bag he had been carrying as he brushed the snow off of the coat and boots. "Sorry about messing up your floors."

"It is just linoleum. It will all just dry up. Come in, you must be frozen." Maddie hung the coat, hat, and scarf in the bathroom. "Can I make you something hot to drink?"

Sy was already holding the dog. "It's a she," as he smiled broadly. "Do you want me to show you the difference?"

She laughed, already taken with the tall man with friendly gestures. "I already figured that much out. Thank you just the same."

"I don't want to impose but some hot chocolate would be most appreciated."

"Have you had dinner yet?"

"No, although I have things back at the house."

"Please let me make you something to go with the chocolate. It is the least that I can do for your kindness. Besides, with all of this confusion I haven't had a chance to eat."

His broad smile warmed her heart. Strange how things work out at times. A lost dog brought her a find.

While she prepared a modest salad, he examined the dog closely. It was difficult to determine her age, but because she was missing some teeth he thought she was not too young. His guess was that she was a terrier mix. He pulled two bowls out of the bag he had brought with him, filling one with a little water and the other with a small amount of dry dog food that was in a pouch. He placed the bowls on the floor in the kitchen and put a training pad close by just in case. The dog, being warm and dry, seemed content at this point to just be held. Maddie could certainly relate to that.

Sy was completely enchanted by the cute petite woman with a charming French accent. He had thought of the librarian stereotype and had expected an unattractive prudish woman. He should really know better than to adhere to stereotypes as they were constantly being proven to be incorrect. This was now finally fully ingrained in him. For him personally as well as for his teaching, preconceived notions can be wrong and even dangerous.

He held the dog as Maddie set out two plates of salad at the side of the cups of hot chocolate. They chatted and the atmosphere was relaxed. Sitting at the table, Sy let the dog lay in his lap believing the human contact was vital. "Many people fail to realize that animals have feelings."

"That is probably due to limited exposure and experience with them. I was brought up in New York City. The apartment building we lived in did not allow animals. The little girl has really bonded with you." She almost added that the big girl had also.

"I have a way with animals. That is why I started out wanting to be a veterinarian."

"What made you change your mind?"

"My father is a lawyer. He finally swayed me. I also have a history of not really knowing from one moment to the next what I want to do."

"You are very young to be a law professor."

"It's just the classic case of being in the right place at the right time. The University wanted to start a special program in the law school on legal journalism. I happened to have started a legal newspaper when I was in law school and branched out with it upon graduation. It is a form of advocacy that can be quite challenging and satisfying. I was invited here to launch the program, and it sounded appealing so I thought I would give it a whirl. You are awfully young to be a librarian."

"Just the classic case of early exposure developing into a self driven dream. Books are my passion."

"Have you been doing this for awhile?"

"No. Just started. This is my first job."

He chuckled. "Two beginners. We have more in common than just dogs. The meal is great, especially considering you just threw it together."

"You know I am French. Food, its preparation and participation is part of my ancestry."

"I brought a leash. Let me try to take the dog out. She probably won't go as she is leery of the snow and there are no clear spaces with the way the wind is blowing the snow around. But, it might be worth a try." He bundled up, but the dog was too smart or too afraid to go out into the elements. Sy carried her out but to no avail. Once back inside, the dog ran straight for the blanket. "As long as I am covered up, I better get back. I have my own little one to cater to. I am sure the University will be closed tomorrow. I'll check with you in the morning to see how you are getting along."

"You have been a big help. Thank you so very much."

"Thank you for the food and drink. Rescuing people in distress is one of my specialties."

She smiled. "I can see why. You're good at it."

"Maybe I will send you a bill."

"If you do, I will have to charge you for the meal."

"I should have guessed. We are even." He extended his hand and grasped the small warm hand she offered. "Nice meeting you, Maddie."

"Likewise, Sy."

She stared at the closed door for a moment after he left. A novel sensation surged through her, and she suspected that her life had just changed drastically.

Maddie went directly to the telephone to call Marie to make sure she got home safely and to tell her of the details of a dream taking shape. Marie's response was predictable. "Only a romantic can turn a blizzard into a bonanza!"

If thou must love me, let it be for naught
Except for love's sake only. Do not say
"I love her for her smile – her look – her way
Of speaking gently, – for a trick of thought
That falls in well with mine, and certes brought
A sense of pleasant ease on such a day" –
For these things in themselves, Beloved, may
Be changed. Change for thee, – and love, so wrought,
May be unwrought so. Neither love me forecast
*   Thine own dear pity's wiping my cheeks dry, –*
*   A creature might forget to weep, who bore*

Thy comfort long, and lose thy love thereby!
But love me for love's sake, that evermore
Thou mayst love on, through love's eternity.

— Elizabeth Barrett Browning

SEVENTEEN

It stopped snowing during the night, although the unabated wind produced such snow-driven conditions it seemed as if it was still snowing. As Sy had predicted, the University was closed for the day and all were advised to stay put except for emergencies and for trips to the cafeteria. The academic buildings were locked down.

Maddie had spent a fitful night as she kept checking on the dog who was content to stay put on the blanket. Whoever the owner was, the dog appeared to be well trained and was well behaved and responsive. Yet, it was such a new experience for Maddie she was nervous and unsure whether the right things were being done. There was also a certain amount of anxiety about the inception of feelings for Sy and whether such were true and if there was any reciprocation. Until he called, a nagging doubt would fester within her.

It was mid-morning when the telephone rang. His tone was upbeat. "How's your border today?"

"Doggone, I can't really tell. She seems to be doing better than I am. I am a nervous wreck."

"Just go with the flow."

"Did you ever hear of a flow going in many different directions?"

He chuckled. "Must be a Library flow. Anyway, you have the luxury of choosing which direction you wish to go."

"I sure could use some advice."

"I'll come over in a bit and check on developments personally."

"Come for lunch."

"You can't just keep on feeding me."

"Why not?"

"I'll get spoiled."

"What's wrong with that?"

"I'll have to think on that.   Perhaps, because the public conception of lawyers is that they are spoiled to begin with, I wouldn't want to enhance that perception. I called the vet's office. No one has called about losing a dog, and the lady I talked to could not match my description with any of their clients but they see many dogs."

"So, where do we go from here?"

"I suppose it is one of those wait and see situations."

"There is something scary about wait and see situations."

"Can also be rewarding. You did save the little girl's life, and it will be heart-warming to reunite her with her owner. Maybe there will even be a monetary reward."

"That is the wait part. For the seeing part, I'll believe it when I see it."

"Have the grounds people shoveled your entrance area?"

"Not yet. Once they do, I'll try taking her out."

"I'll come over now.   She must have to go, and I'll try it."

"You sure are helpful."

"I'm trying to build up international relations."

Maddie imposed in her mind that he meant personal relations, which was fine with her. "I'll make some coffee if you drink that."

"I do. That will be great, and have that instead of lunch."

The coffee was just about brewed when there was a knock on the door. His smile was wide and warm, and as he entered Maddie instinctively hugged him. She already had the dog on the leash, so he took her out while he was still dressed for the elements. In ten minutes he was back and the dog had not relieved herself.

Maddie served toast with orange marmalade with the coffee. He drank the coffee black just as she did, and for her the list of things they had in common just kept growing. "Are you in a serious relationship?" She had not planned to ask this question, but it just came out.

"No. I haven't dated much since college. Law school was far too demanding and whatever spare time I did have went toward newspaper activities. I did have a college sweetheart. I thought that was the real thing. Yet, as we grew our desires and expectations diverged. Then, it was as if I reverted back to my teen years when I was overly shy with girls. One of the frustrating things I had to deal with and which made it awkward and rather uncomfortable being with a girl was that my palms sweated profusely. My hands were so clammy I didn't dare to try and hold a girl's hand, and if I did they would recoil at my touch. Growing up can be painful."

"For girls as well. You should talk to my friend, Marie, who teaches in the English Department. She has some experiences that have left emotional scars. She is writing a book on these problems youngsters have to face."

"I could give her more material and insight, for sure. Are you in a serious relationship?"

"No, unfortunately. I have had boyfriends over the years, but there always seemed to be something missing. It just did not feel right. Maybe I am seeking too much. My career is so satisfying I naturally want a love to match it."

"Sounds reasonable."

"Are your palms sweating now?"

He laughed. "I've outgrown that, probably too late for it to have done any good."

Not knowing where her forwardness was coming from, she reached for his hand. "Let's see. I'm a girl."

"I noticed."

His hand was not even damp. In fact, it was soft and warm. It was evident that he had not done any hard labor in his life. An intellectual's resume. "How does it feel to be all grown up?"

"I am not sure I am fully grown."

"Why do you say that?"

"I have a gnawing feeling, almost a seething mystery, that there is something else I need to do in life. I suppose I will figure it out one day. Then, and probably only then, can I declare that I am grown up."

"You have accomplished much so far. Maybe if you dwell on this, it is enough."

"Maybe. Yet, the feeling is there and I am not sure I can talk it or even think it away."

"My friend, Marie, has the same sensation. She believes it is the book she needs to write. You should talk to her."

"Might be helpful. I have tried talking to others I thought receptive of the notion, including my father, but they all seem to dismiss it as a form of uncertainty that will pass in time. I think the more people belittle it, the more important it becomes to me. Sorry to sound so serious, but you did ask."

"I have an idea. Marie and I have become good friends. We have this enjoyable ritual of exchanging Saturday night dinners that we prepare. It is not only food we share. We have had a number of probing conversations, and it sounds as if you would fit right in. This Saturday it is my turn to host the dinner here. Why don't you join us?"

"Sounds intriguing and mighty kind of you. Can I bring anything?"

"Marie is also French so French wine is a staple."

"I can handle that."

He left shortly afterward. Maddie played with the dog until they both fell asleep on the sofa. When she got up, the urge to write a poem about and for Sy took a firm hold. Another positive sign. First, however, since the entrance area had now been shoveled, she took the dog out. Either because the area was clear or she was more relaxed, the dog relieved herself right away. Maddie was amazed that she had held it all in for so long.

Staring out of the window at the expansive snow-covered scene, her mind raced in many directions. The poem would settle her restless spirit.

Even a well defined path offers meanderings at a time,
A surprise turn can lead to vast fortunes for the spirit;
It can prompt a travel that excites and a destination sublime,
And, of course, you never know until you try it.

A chance meeting along the way can inflame the heart,

No plan can predict it, no clue allowing one to prepare;
A new phase in a life scheme is about to start,
With thoughts, emotions, and experiences to share.

She tore the sheet of paper out of the notebook, folded it, and then kissed it. A satisfied smile came to her lips followed by a wink to the dog. It was a wonderful day reflecting a highly promising future.

There is a Smile of Love
And there is a Smile of Deceit
And there is a Smile of Smiles
In which these two Smiles meet

— William Blake

EIGHTEEN

It was back to work on the next day. The grounds of the University were a winter wonderland. Snow drifts piled high resembled castles. Blowing snow still covered the earlier cleared walkways and were visualized as carpets to the castles. Maddie contrasted the pristine condition of the snow with the snow that falls in New York City which turns to a dirty slush within hours. As much as she loved city living, perhaps its was merely what she was accustomed to. There was much to tout about the features of rural conditions, although she was now of the opinion that there were pros and cons for wherever one was.

There was still no missing dog report, although Harry and Will were making inquiries in many places. The only thing Maddie could do was as Sy had advised and wait and see what developed. Meanwhile, she was becoming quite attached to the little creature, and planned to go home at lunch time to walk her.

Marie dropped by and offered to help. Her suggestions were to put up some missing dog signs around town and to put a notice in the campus newspaper. She was also looking forward to Saturday night and to meeting Sy. Marie was quite aware of the twinkle in Maddie's eyes.

Sy also came by, not only to see where she worked but also to tell her that he made an appointment with the Veterinarian on Saturday morning so the dog could be checked out. He knew she did not have a car and offered to drive her there. Maddie had to add thoughtfulness to the growing list of Sy's attributes. He ventured to say that he had a favor to ask while they were in town. He wanted to stop at the store so that she could select the right wine. She responded that was fine and that she could then pick up some fresh items for the dinner at the same time.

Maddie received an elated greeting from the dog when she arrived at the middle of the day. The dog went right away when she took her out. Maddie had a yogurt sitting on the sofa as the dog lay by her side. She filled the bowl with fresh water before she headed back to the Library. All of this exercise would help to keep the weight off.

The week ended without a single inquiry about the dog. Baffled by it all, Maddie knew she was approaching a dilemma. She was not only getting used to having the dog around, she liked it. How could the owner not miss such a gentle and loving animal? The experience with Nate steeled her for strange occurrences that life can foster, but it would be difficult to decide whether to keep the dog or to find another home for her. Harry had two dogs already, so he was not a likely candidate. Maddie could post a looking for a home note at various places.

On Friday evening Sy came over with his dog, Cally, a mixed breed hound. They walked the dogs together, although the cold kept them from wandering too far. The dogs seemed to get along just fine, and after telling him her thoughts about the dog he offered to take her. He was already a committed dog person. In the meantime, he suggested they exchange keys and on alternate days at lunch they could each come home and walk the two dogs. If a week ago someone were to tell her that she was about to meet a wonderful man as well as take in a stray dog, she would not have believed it. No wonder the vagaries of life are tempting topics for poetry and prose.

Maddie figured she should give the dog a name. It was awkward and bothersome to refer to her as the dog. It was probably not the kind of name most people would think of as suitable, but she named her *Blizzard* after the event of their meeting. Marie thought something French would be better although she liked the name given. Sy also liked it, and he joked that if she used a nickname such as Blizzy it sounded French.

The next day's visit to the Veterinarian went well, although Maddie was a bit shocked how expensive it turned out to be. Her

Forever Old, Forever New

budget certainly had not made provision for pet care. The Vet estimated Blizzard's age to be around six, mainly from the condition of the teeth. She had been neutered and appeared healthy in all respects. Basic shots were given just in case. Maddie put up a notice in the waiting room about a found dog, and she admittedly had mixed feelings about anticipated results.

They went to the food store. Sy stayed in the car with Blizzard while Maddie picked up the things she needed, including the French wine on Sy's behalf. He then dropped them off as she needed the time left in the day for preparation of the meal.

Marie arrived early as she was anxious to hear all about Sy before she actually met him. She also brought a bottle of wine, so it was plain to see that even if the meal did not turn out to be the best that there was plenty of wine to wash it down with.

The veal parmigiana with roasted mushrooms turned out to be a delight to all. The wine was enjoyable and the conversation robust. Blizzard stayed clear from the talkative folks as she desired a quiet space. Because of that, they theorized that Blizzard's owner was probably a single person and that there were no children around.

Sy and Marie were swept up in many common experiences and behavioral patterns. Most notable was the characteristic they shared of being impatient with achievements. Both had a similar track record of trying various activities and once excelling at them then quickly tiring of them and abandoning them. Ideas were easily exchanged as well. Marie offered journalistic suggestions, and Sy had some enterprising thoughts concerning the contents of her opus. Maddie was slightly jealous of their mutual compatibility, but she was not the kind of person to be angry or annoyed. It was eye-opening to realize that because of her young age and limited expansive experiences she had little to add to deep analysis and as to the whys and wherefores of life. She listened intently as this was a good way to learn.

As the evening progressed Sy realized that he had more in common with Marie than with Maddie. While he was taken initially with Maddie's attractive youthfulness Marie was the person he might get close to, even romantically, discounting that she was older than he was.

Marie was taken with Sy's serious demeanor and provocative thinking. She knew how Maddie felt, and she would not want to hurt her for the world. Yet, she knew Maddie would respect an honesty that close friendship breeds and that there might be potential for her coupling with Sy. As painful as reality might be at times it has to be faced head on.

Sy and Marie left at the same time, and Maddie suspected that the evening was not done for them. Maddie had to admit she was a little disappointed and probably had a right to be that way. She sat on the sofa with Blizzard sound asleep on her lap as she drained the remaining wine in the glass. She was not too young to philosophize that what she thought might be was not meant to be. She just needed to be patient and alert for what was out there to take its place. In the meantime, the dog was more comfort than she ever would have realized.

The day is cold, and dark, and dreary;
It rains, and the wind is never weary;
The vine still clings to the mouldering wall,
But at every gust the dead leaves fall,
And the day is dark and dreary.

My life is cold, and dark, and dreary;
It rains, and the wind is never weary;
My thoughts still cling to the mouldering Past,
But the hopes of youth fall thick in the blast,
And the days are dark and dreary.

Be still, sad heart! and cease repining;
Behind the clouds is the sun still shining;
Thy fate is the common fate of all,
Into each life some rain must fall,
Some days must be dark and dreary.

— Henry Wadsworth Longfellow

NINETEEN

It was early Sunday afternoon when Marie telephoned. "I'll be right over." She hung up before Maddie could usher any response.

As soon as she entered she flung her arms around Maddie hugging her tightly. "Can you ever forgive me? I am so, so sorry."

"I'm not."

Marie broke away, staring deeply into Maddie's eyes. "You're not?"

Maddie took Marie's coat and put it over the bench by the door and led her to the sofa. Blizzard faithfully jumped up onto her lap. "You have nothing to be sorry about. I saw it coming, and strangely it felt right for you both. I am learning lessons through first-hand experiences. My newest lesson is that acceptance is the key to forgiveness."

"For one so young, you are very wise."

"Obviousness is ageless."

"Proves my point. Another wise assertion."

"We are friends, and I know you did nothing to hurt me intentionally."

"For sure. We went to his place and talked for hours. It is almost scary how much we have in common. I have not felt this way, initially, with anyone. It may not lead to anything, and with my track record I would be alright with that. It is a pleasure stop on a painful highway. As much as I wanted him to, he did not even try to kiss me."

Maddie chuckled. "Please spare me the details. I have loved

and lost and do not need any reminders."

"You are one wonderful person, mademoiselle. I am so grateful to have you in my life."

"Likewise. Sy and I were not meant to be. What is meant to be is still out there, and I am counting on you enjoying it with me when it happens."

Marie hugged her forcefully. "For sure."

"So, tell me what is the thing you feel you have the most in common with Sy?"

Marie thought for a moment. "It is probably what I call the give up syndrome."

"I can't wait to hear this!"

"We both like to, and actually have, tried many pursuits or interests and once mastering them then completely abandon them as if they never existed. For example, he took up painting. He took lessons, bought all of the equipment and painted a series of landscapes and seascapes. Then he gave it up completely and just gave away all of the canvases. I suppose one might say we have a wayward spirit in tandem."

"Does that mean you are going to give up poetry?"

"I dare say it is in the cards eventually. I sense that once I finish the book, if ever, I'll go on to something completely different."

"How about teaching?"

"Too fresh, too soon to hazard a guess as to what might happen. I'll tire of it, the enthusiasm will go, most likely."

"How about Sy?"

"That's not a pursuit. That's a love drive, and it has a different set of rules. It can go either way."

"I am giving him up so that you can give him up?"

"I didn't say the rules were fair."

"What about me?"

"Some friendships are forever."

"That saves you from a more concentrated lecture. The weakness you describe, seems to me, can be simply cured by mind over matter. Exploration and experimentation are separate and apart from a sincere involvement. That can and should be lasting. Otherwise, nothing would be worth lasting."

"Perhaps. Oh, wise one."

Later in the afternoon Maddie walked Blizzard over to Sy's place. She knocked on the door, and he smiled and invited them in. After she took off her coat he hugged her. "Sure was a feast last night. Thanks for including me."

"You added much to the evening. Marie has told me everything."

"Good. I want us to be good friends."

"We already are. In fact, I brought a spare key so we can share the dog walking."

"Fine. Can I make you some coffee?"

"No, thanks. I just finished lunch. But, you can show me around. Marie said you have many intriguing pieces."

"Sure enough. My parents are avid antiques collectors, and they let me take some pieces that I like to give the place a homey feeling. All of it will be mine someday."

"I know zilch about antiques except for old books but I am eager to learn as much as possible about things I don't know."

"Antiques are like books. No one can know about them all. Maybe, that is part of the allure. Being involved with a certain category of antiques, as with books, can lead to a certain degree of expertise while other categories remain a mystery. Since my parents included me at a young age in all of their hunts, what I know I picked up from them."

For close to an hour Sy showed her the various items scattered around the place. Maddie could tell he enjoyed talking about them, and if one had a story with it he embellished it accordingly. When she left, the thought lingered on the entire walk home that it was too bad she was not as lucky as Marie.

For all of the sad words of tongue and pen,
The saddest are these: 'It might have been!'

Ah, well! For us all some sweet hope lies
Deeply buried from human eyes;

And, in the hereafter, angels may
Roll the stone from its grave away!

— John Greenleaf Whittier

TWENTY

On Monday morning Maddie was engrossed in making entries in the computer at her desk when the Head Librarian, Constance Gilford, came in. "I have a special favor to ask of you."

Maddie looked up at the matronly lady and detected a weariness in her face. "Sure."

"Professor Poindexter in the Philosophy Department has requested an obscure book that is in your part of the collections. You may not know about Professor Poindexter, but he is probably the oldest member of the faculty and is confined to a wheelchair. He is paramount in his field and one of the University's prized assets. He has been here for well over forty years. Anyway," handing Maddie an index card, "This is the book and I would like you to take it over to him. He will be in his office, 312 Adams, from eleven to twelve. That is the only building with an elevator."

"I'll be glad to do it."

"Thanks," as she turned and left.

The book was not only obscure it was very old. Maddie located it in the stacks without any problem, but it was evident that it had not been handled for a long time. The copyright date was 1810, and the pages were brown and quite brittle. Bringing it back to her office, she placed it in a protective plastic sleeve, put a handle with care sticker on the sleeve, and made a notation in the loan section on the computer of the date and borrower.

When she knocked on the heavy wood door of Professor Poindexter's office, he bellowed, "Well, come in for darn sake."

She opened the door, and it was a sight to behold. Professor Poindexter had a full head of white hair and the glasses were well down on a long narrow nose on a wrinkled face. He was in the wheelchair which was under the long table apparently used as his desk. The table was cluttered with papers and high piles of books. She sensed that only he could know where anything was and what he was doing. The walls were noticeably barren except for one large striking framed photograph of a gorgeous rainbow arching from mountains.

Upon seeing the young woman in the doorway, he grunted. "Can't you read? The sign says student consulting hours are three to four. When are you young people going to fit into the real world?"

Maddie closed the door behind her. Her voice was sharper than it probably should be to her usual show of respect to those older than she and those in a higher position. "I am not a student. I am Maddie Ponte from the Collections Department of the Library and I have brought the book you are interested in."

"Well, why didn't you say so?"

"I just did."

"Bring it here, child. Librarians are getting younger all the time. I swear young folk are taking over the world and one of the reasons the world is in deep trouble. All of this is to the dismay of old timers."

Handing the book to him, her voice was stern. "I put it in a plastic sleeve as it is quite fragile. I trust you will keep it safe."

He grunted again. "I trust I know what to do with old books." He looked at her intently and he had many years of experience to rely on in evaluating that this young woman was alert and most likely quite bright. "French, aren't you?"

"Obvious does as obvious is."

"Ornery, too."

"Only when the occasion calls for it."

"Sit down, lass. You make me nervous looking down your nose at me. I have a gruff bark but a gentle bite, I assure you. Besides, I need to pick your brain."

She smiled, took off her coat and sat in a chair across the table from him. "That will cost you extra."

He was fond of grunting. Grunting covers many fronts. "I'll

determine whether there is any value in the picking."

"Librarians are known for retaliating."

"My brain has been picked over so many times only a few crumbs are left."

"Humble, too, I see."

He sure liked this feisty youngster. Banter was one of the few enjoyments he had left. "Humble pie is my lunch staple."

"Speaking of lunch I have to get home to walk my dog. So, you better make the picking fast."

"What kind of dog is it?"

After relating a capsulized version of events, she closed forcefully, "Aren't you sorry you asked?"

"Not in the least. You are smart enough to know that." He noted her intent stare at the picture of the rainbow. "Hauntingly beautiful, isn't it?"

"Yes. I have never seen a real one."

"You are missing a magnificent sight. A picture does not do it justice. Some day I may tell you its true meaning. Anyway, did you have a dream last night?"

She wondered why a rainbow would be important to him, but dismissed the thought as something she would never find out about. "I dreamed that a gruff old man wanted to psychoanalyze me."

"Librarian retaliation duly noted. Now, seriously, answer my question."

She watched the stern look on his face and admitted to herself that she should be more respectful. "Strange you should want to know that. I have vivid dreams. Besides being a librarian I am an amateur poet and have always believed that poets have more significant and detailed dreams than most other people."

"Imagination conquers reality."

"Not always."

"There is no such thing as always. Philosophers discerned that long ago. Anatole France aptly said *To know is nothing at all; to imagine is everything*"

"You have written many books. Are any on dreams?"

"Let's get back to that. What did you dream about last night?"

"Love."

"That sure is a broad area."

"Inspired by my thinking tempered with a recent real life situation I met the man to fulfill my desires only to lose him to a friend."

"Then he really wasn't the man of your dreams. That man would not have left you."

"That is one way to look at it."

"So, in effect, you dreamed about the lost one or the one to be found?"

"It bounced back and forth."

"Imagination conquering reality."

"There must be an echo in here. I have heard that before. Why are you so interested in dreams, anyway?"

"In due time, child. If youngsters only had half the patience of seniors."

"Then answer me this, do dreams come true?"

Another grunt. "You already know nobody can answer that question. But, for you as an individual you certainly can try to make it so. Yet, why not just enjoy the dream for dream sake?"

"Because I will eventually wake up and have to face a world I have no control over."

"Are you sure about that?"

"What do you mean?"

"Many go through life with eyes, ears, and heart closed. They might just as well be asleep."

"I am not that way," a defiant tone matching her words.

"I didn't say anything about you. Rather defensive, aren't you?"

"It is a sensitive subject."

"Too bad I am too old for you. Between your volatility and my stubbornness we are a good fit. Besides, I am already married."

"I feel sorry for her. If she is not getting questions she is getting grunts."

He laughed. "Good one, lass. My first chuckle of the day, nay the month. My wife calls me the Gruntmeister."

She stood and put on her coat. "I really have to go, but why did you want to know what I dreamed last night?"

"Just a theory I am exploring. I like to think I recognize a dreamer when I see one."

"What did you dream about last night?"

"That I was about to ask a beautiful French woman about her dreams. See, perhaps dreams do come true."

"You sure are a loveable Gruntmeister."

"Nice of you to notice. When will you come back to visit me?"

"Here is my card with my direct number. Call me when you want me to take the book back."

"A dreaming librarian. What a dichotomy!"

Walking home, Maddie kept thinking what a delightful person the professor was. She could probably learn a great deal from him. Besides her parents, she did not know much about old people. Her exposure to them had been limited, and she was thinking she might have missed out on much. It was a mystery what old people think about and feel. It was long overdue for her to enter that arena.

And if I should live to be
The last leaf upon the tree
In the spring,
Let them smile, as I do now,
At the old forsaken bough
Where I cling.

— Oliver Wendell Holmes

TWENTY ONE

At her office early the next morning, Maddie did a computer search on Professor Elliot Poindexter. What she was able to retrieve was basically just his academic record and faculty standing. Nothing of a personal nature could be found other than his age of seventy-nine and that he was married. Maddie knew just where to go to find out more. She telephoned Harry. Harry was, as she had already discovered through his long tenure at the college a walking encyclopedia on the who, when, and why of the college and its people. In addition to that, he loved to espouse the stories he heard and other tidbits he had discovered or put together from a host of sources.

Elliot Poindexter had come to Blantyre when he was thirty-two years of age. He had already received his Doctorate of Philosophy but had always refused to be addressed as Dr. Poindexter. Besides his high intelligence, his social and academic radical ideas fit right in with Blantyre tradition. He had already written three books, all well received in the academic world despite their divergence from staid theories. He had been teaching at a college in the deep South fighting ignorance as well as racial hatred when Blantyre snatched him away. Three years later, on a snowy day, his infant son had severe breathing problems so he was rushing him to the hospital. His wife and the boy were in the back seat. The car skidded on a patch of ice hidden beneath the snow, rolled over and slammed into a tree. His wife and son were killed and the professor was trapped in the car with crushed legs. It was hours before rescue freed him, and by the time they got him to the hospital he had hypothermia and because of his injuries both legs had to be amputated. Any ordinary person would have been destroyed by such events, but Professor Poindexter is no ordinary man. He took a leave of absence for a year. Nobody knew where he was or what he was doing. To this day it is still a mystery. Of course, rumors were rampant and ranged from him drinking constantly or being on drugs to contemplation and failed attempts at suicide. The professor apparently has never talked about it with anyone. Upon his return, he tackled the field of philosophy with a vengeance. He wrote a series of articles further attacking the most accepted thinking and theories, and he quickly gained the reputation among the students of being the most demanding member of the faculty. At any other college students would have avoided signing up for his classes. Here, the students welcomed the challenge and flooded his classes where they reveled in saying they learned more there than anywhere else. Each year, he hired a student to live with him in his Tudor house just outside of town to assist him in his daily routines as well as to serve as a research assistant. Those students never revealed anything. Some ten years later he hired a female student, and by the end of the school year they were married. Nobody has ever known the story behind that or what has gone on behind closed doors. She has been with him ever since. She is a bit of a mystery woman. She takes him to the college every day and picks him up at the end of the day. She is by his side when needed, but speaks rarely and does not participate in faculty wives' events or any of the college proceedings. There has always been gossip about her, the marriage, and the age difference. As far as Harry was concerned whatever people do is fine with him as long as it does not hurt others. He added emphatically that it was also none of his bee's wax.

Maddie's response to the revelation was emphatic. "Wow! That sure is some story!"

"Just one more story in the naked city."

"Confirms my initial impression that he is a fascinating man."

"Join the club. Many are of the same opinion."

"I would like to get to know him better."

"It is said he does not let people get close to him."

"I'm not a people. I am a caring Librarian."

"Tell me something I don't already know."

It was mid-afternoon when she glanced up at the open doorway to the office. A woman was leaning against the door frame and there was something familiar about her. It was Honore, but she had changed her hair style and she was dressed in jeans with a baggy sweatshirt so at first she did not appear like the earlier visitor. Maddie stood up. "Come in, Honore."

The alluring young woman smiled and swiftly moved to the chair by the side of the desk. "I'm glad you remember me."

Maddie sat down and peered into the hazel eyes. "Why would I forget you?"

"I represented a shock to your being."

"I was not shocked, just not interested."

"Be that as it may. I am on to other things now."

Maddie felt a surge of relief and immediately relaxed. "Good for you."

Honore had a sly smile on her face. "No, good for you. You are too pretty to have resisted me for long if I persisted."

Maddie thought it best just to ignore that remark. "So, this is not a social visit?"

"Kinda"

"Kinda what?"

"Professor Foundelet mentioned to me that you are a poet."

Maddie smiled. "Not a poet of her caliber. I am an amateur, what I would call just a dabbler in the art form."

"Professor Foundelet is quite inspiring. I had never tried my hand at poetry, although I have read many poems over the years. I guess I just never had a reason to write a poem. Anyway, she has given us an assignment to write a short poem, any style, any subject. I found it easy to do, maybe too easy. Before I hand it in I hope you will give me your opinion on it." She handed Maddie a sheet of paper on which the poem was hand-written. The first thing Maddie noted was that Honore had beautiful handwriting.

"I'm not sure I am the best person to do this, but I'll give it a shot." She held the paper firmly as she read.

ODE TO A FUTURELESS FUTURE

I gaze out beyond the here and now –
  I see, perhaps, things I am not meant to see –
There are repression, hunger, poverty, sickness –
  A world I would like to avoid but can't ignore –
My instinct is to want to change it all –
  My intellect tells me it is a futile task –
So, if the chips are down, do I listen –
  To my mind or my heart? –
But, if it is the latter, where do I start?

Maddie handed the paper back. "I like it, although it is rather depressing. Is that actually the way you feel?"

"Certainly, many of us do. How can you plan for a future when there may not be one?"

"But, there might be. If there turns out to be a future how can you handle it if you have not planned for it?"

"And, if not, all of that wasted energy."

"How can anything you do for yourself and about yourself be wasted?"

"If it has no use, no purpose."

"Professor Foundelet would want to hear these thoughts you have. She is writing a book about all of this. Do you know that?"

"She has mentioned about writing a book, but has not said what it is about. What do you think about the future?"

"Everyday of my life is preparation for the future. I am guarding and preserving this treasure house of the written word for all tomorrows. I am guiding and encouraging research into the wisdom of the past to be used in the future. The ills of the world do not condemn it. Rather, they represent the challenge for better governments, better societies, better people, and better ideas."

"You should be a teacher."

"As with learning, not all teaching takes place in the classroom."

A thought of reference to Professor Poindexter streaked through her mind.

Honore stood up. "I better go. Thanks for your help. I'll think about what you said."

"Thanks for considering me to help you."

Before passing through the doorway, Honore turned, smiled, and said in an upbeat tone, "And I will think about you."

Though leaves are many, the root is one;
Through all the lying days of my youth
I swayed my leaves and flowers in the sun;
Now I may wither into the truth.

— William Butler Yeats

TWENTY-TWO

It was two days later when Constance stopped by early in the morning with a request for another book for Professor Poindexter. This time he specifically requested that Maddie bring it to him. As the Head Librarian was about to leave, she commented with a tinge of envy, "He has apparently taken a shine to you. It has long been recounted that if he remembers your name he likes you."

Maddie retrieved the book from the stacks. It was another old one in poor condition, so she placed it in a protective plastic sleeve and put it aside for the excursion to the professor's office at eleven o'clock.

She knocked and entered without waiting for a response. Professor Poindexter was turned in the wheelchair and staring out of the window. "Let me guess. It is a young French woman carrying a book."

"Close," she spouted, "It is a young American woman with a French accent holding a book in poor condition which will not be delivered without a promise of utmost care in its use."

He grunted and swiveled around. "I promise under one condition."

"What is that?"

"You sit with an old man for awhile and entertain him."

"Entertaining is not in my job description."

"Well, I will have to see to it that it is revised accordingly."

"I'll be fired since I am not the entertaining type."

"Your name should be Sassy not Maddie."

"Only my friends call me Sassy."

"Ah, but I wish to be your friend."

She placed the book on the table, removed her coat and sat in the chair across from him. "There are no secrets between friends."

A loud grunt, one that undoubtedly could be heard in the hallway. "So, you are as curious as others to poke into my world."

"You are an enigma."

"And proud of it. Let's just talk for now. Some day I may let you in on things others only guess at."

"Did you ever hear of the phrase *false promises?*"

"I have heard of *failed promises.*"

"What do you want to talk about?"

"Tell me about yourself."

"Not as much to tell as I would like. My parents are French. We came to New York City when I was a child. They worked for a French magazine and covered developments at the United Nations. I was raised and schooled in Ethical Culture. Ever hear of that?"

A series of emphatic grunts. "As a matter of fact I have read much about it, and I have even studied Algernon Black's papers. Ethical Culture is an interesting movement in the field of religion. It is not far afield from Humanism, and if you check the holdings in the Library you will see that I wrote two books dealing with Humanism."

"I should have known, or at least guessed that you are conversant in that arena. Anyway, my greatest discovery was the New York Public Library which led me to become a librarian. My special find and delight in that magnificent place were the great poets. That inspired me to become a fledgling poet. That's it in a nut shell. I am young, devoid of substantive experiences, but eager to learn all that I can."

"Are your parents still around?"

"Yes, although they have moved back to Paris. Now, a quid pro quo. Tell me about yourself."

She was sure there would be a grunt, but it was more like a sigh. "Ah, my dear, that is a tough nut to crack."

"You can do it, I am sure. If nothing else, I am good listener."

Then there was the anticipated grunt. "I was the youngest in a large family in upstate New York. My parents had inter-married in an age when that was not only frowned upon but also vilified. The respective families shunned them, even when children arrived. My humanist principles came from my father, an avid reader. I really did not discover books on my own until I was in high school, but unbeknownst to me I was a knowledge gatherer long before that. I was dismissed by adults for asking too many questions. As you know I still ask many questions." Another grunt. "I graduated early from high school and breezed through college and graduate school. I worked to pay my way through and I had many odd jobs. To this day each of these varied jobs added something to my mental and emotional development. That's it. Pretty dull, uh?"

"Not quite."

"My parents and all my siblings are gone, except for a sister in a nursing home in California. I inherited a short life span, so I am here on borrowed time. If the truth be known, I died a long time ago."

"I know about the accident. I am so, so sorry."

She waited for a grunt but there was not one. "There was a lesson in that, too. What is considered a normal life can change in an instant. An event can shatter expectations, hopes, and just about everything else that might keep you going."

"You did put your life back together, didn't you?"

Now came a grunt, a series of them. "No, I never did. You might say I made a new life."

"You don't have to say any more if it is painful."

"The pain is always there, whether I talk about it or not. I sense your compassion, so talking comes easily."

"You are admired and respected here."

"Feared is more apt."

"No wonder you grunt so much. You confuse results with motivation."

He reached his hand across the table. There were tears at the corners of his eyes, plainly visible over the rim of the glasses that had slipped down his nose. "I lost my son. If I ever had a daughter, I would have wanted her to be just like you."

She grasped his hand and did not know what to say or even what she could say. The silence narrated the moment.

Love has earth to which she clings
With hills and circling arms about –
Wall within wall to shut fear out.
But Thought has need of no such things,
For Thought has a pair of dauntless wings.

— Robert Frost

TWENTY-THREE

Marie held the Saturday night dinner, and Maddie was not surprised that Sy was invited. Besides the wonderful stew that she made the evening was engrossing. Marie was fully involved in writing the book, inspired and bolstered by Sy's fascinating stories and unusual experiences. The two freely exchanged thoughts throughout the meal and afterward. If it was not for the telling of her encounter with Professor Poindexter, Maddie would have been quiet the entire time.

Sy drove Maddie home, and he made no secret that after he dropped her off he was headed back to Marie's place. She was not bothered by it and only hoped that whatever was developing between them would be worthwhile and lasting since they both openly admitted they tired of things quickly. They would have to work on enduring elements.

Maddie walked Blizzard, but a brisk cold wind had them back in the warmth of the house after they had gone only a short distance. Once inside, Maddie curled up on the sofa with Blizzard by her side. The dog fell asleep immediately while Maddie tried to get interested in the book she held. She found it difficult to concentrate as her thoughts branched out in many directions. Should she withdraw from the Saturday night ritual to afford the couple maximum time to be alone? Should she still seek another home for Blizzard? Should she continue visits with Professor Poindexter? Such visits might be good for her as she could learn much from the astute scholar. Yet, it might not be good for him as he was already agonizing over her as a daughter that he might have had. Should she be receptive to any further discussions with Honore? Should she finally go out on a date with Will as he has urged so often? There were no easy answers, and Maddie concluded for the moment that it would be best to see if any of the situations worked out for themselves.

All of the uncertainties carried through the night, and Maddie kept waking up. Not a conducive manner for dreaming.

On Sunday, she spent the morning cleaning and the afternoon catching up on communications.   Her friends were involved in an assortment of interesting ventures, and she was keen on keeping track of them all.   Careers were blossoming, marriages transpiring, and families established.   Many attributed an Ethical Culture connection and schooling to enhancing and appreciating accomplishments.   She had not heard from one friend, Sally Edwards, for some time so it was with some excitement that Maddie opened Sally's letter, particularly since it had a return address in Africa.

Maddie, my dear friend –

Forgive me for not being in contact for a long time.   I have thought of you often, and there are many moments I recall the rewards of our friendship throughout our years at school.   I obtained your current address from Rochelle Altman, and she has told me of your current position, and it sounds like a dream job for you.   I am sure you are enjoying it and making great strides.

For the past four years I have been working for the African Wildlife Foundation, an organization headquartered in the United States but active throughout Africa to ensure the wildlife and wild lands of Africa will endure forever.   I am now in my fifth African nation, and I have been exposed to many aspects of this endeavor, both good and terribly bad.   I dare say my youth has been enhanced and tarnished all at the same time if that makes any sense at all.   Amidst seething civil unrest and abject poverty inherent in this continent, some love the animals and are enthralled in watching them run free, while others look at animals only as a potential source of revenue and encourage hunting and poaching. Africa itself presents a stark and almost eery beauty. It is difficult to explain, but the longer I am here the more I love it and hate it.

At times, I think of a "normal" life I may be missing back in the States. Yet, I feel I am doing some good here and as difficult as the mission is I am bound to the dedicated people I work with. Sickness and poisonous animals are ever present dangers, not to mention that portion of the population who resent our presence and deeds. My parents worry about me and feel I have done enough. I suppose I will come to that same conclusion eventually, but I am not yet at that point.

I recall our school days, and perhaps I did not make enough of the opportunities back then. Hindsight is true sight. I don't want to feel that way again. I value our friendship from those days. Some declared you were too serious, but I admired your steadiness and thirst for knowledge. I bask in the warm memories of our long personal conversations. I am sure you are doing wonders at the college. Be well, and enjoy all of those books.

Your forever friend,

Sally

Maddie pulled out a piece of University stationary, stared out of the window, and rubbed her chin. The response then took form.

Sally, my admired friend:

Your letter and the descriptions of your actions and surroundings brought tears and joy to my eyes and heart. Young people are often of the opinion they cannot change the world. You are doing that, and I can boast that my friend is doing that. My wishes for success and safety are sent with this letter.

I recently found a lost dog, nobody has claimed her, and she has brought a new insight for me about animals. They have feelings and need care, attention, and protection as do people. I envision you working in that field here as well when and if you return.

Each day at the University is a learning experience for me. The expanded world of books is my passion, and through my fortunate association with others I have gained perspective about others and their dreams. A professor writing a book to bolster thoughts and desires of young people is using me as a sounding board. An elderly professor has unwittingly become my mentor and has opened my eyes not only to the humanity of older folks but also as to the extent of their sacrifices. The road to old age can be arduous, but with planning and the right attitude it can be a wonderful and worthwhile journey.

I have not been dating as the eligible bachelor field is limited. Most of the faculty are married and I am not allowed to socialize with the students. I don't know if you knew Will Alexander. He was two years ahead of us at school. He is a graduate student here and also a campus police officer. No romantic interest on my part but our backgrounds prompt a comforting friendship. In my book of life romance may be on the next page.

Stay in touch, and be well and safe. Hugs across the many miles.

Maddie

Maddie was glad Sy had given her a dog sweater for Blizzard. She put it on her and they walked further than they had done earlier. Upon returning to the warmth of the home she fed Blizzard and then herself, took a shower and went to sleep. She would welcome a dream to tell the professor about.

The sense of the world is short,
Long and various the report,
To love and be beloved;
Men and gods have not unlearned it,
And how oft soe'er they've turned it,
'Tis not to be improved.

— Ralph Waldo Emerson

TWENTY-FOUR

When Maddie arrived at her office on Tuesday morning there was a telephone message from Professor Poindexter. He was finished with the books he had on loan and asked her to come at eleven to pick them up. He also asked her to bring her wits, hits, and misses with her.

"Come in, little lady," Professor Poindexter bellowed when Maddie knocked on the door.

"Good day, Gruntmeister."

He grunted right on cue. "Take off your coat. The books are ready for your transport, but let's chat for a spell."

"Hits, misses, or wits?"

"All in bits."

She put her coat on a chair and sat across the table from him. Noticing a stain on his old worn tie, she could not restrain herself on commenting about it. "Part of your breakfast is on your tie."

Another grunt, not unexpected. "A purposeful focal point so that others will have to look at me. I can't remember which meal escaped from my mouth. One of my misses, I suppose."

Maddie laughed. "The only miss. Doesn't really matter, does it?"

"What does matter, little lady?"

"For the moment or the long haul?"

"Both. By the way, we are now friends so dispense with calling me Professor or Gruntmeister. I am Elliott."

"Alright, Elliott. You are the philosopher extraordinaire. You tell me the difference between what matters for the here and now and what matters tomorrow."

"Totally subjective, it seems to me. Many of the important features have blurry lines separating them."

"If I reveal, in confidence, such conceptualizations, will you respond in kind?"

"You drive a hard bargain. In confidence, of course."

"Of course." She was sure there would be a grunt but none came forth. "One thing I do notice is that you are unpredictable."

"I was going to say the same thing about you. Another mystery shrouding youth and old age."

"Speaking of mysteries, a line by Whittier has always intrigued me. What do you think he meant by *Forever old, forever new*?"

Now came an anticipated grunt. "He probably meant only to paraphrase what we are talking about concerning what matters most to a person. Things that have existed all along become new to you when you discover them. It is a subjective, totally subjective interpretation. He wanted those who read that thought to thoroughly digest it. I am an old buzzard and at the same time a new friend to you. Does that matter?"

"Certainly. And, it is what matters to me now and tomorrow. Your words are the living thoughts of the great poets that I have been enthralled by."

"The teacher in me raises its ugly head. But, they are not my thoughts. It is the mirror I hold for you to see yourself. It is the board I hold so you can hear the echo of your own words. It is the old guiding you to its newness. An apt saying, and excuse the pun, reflects the concept for all of life. It is not how many breaths you take that matters, rather it is the moments that take your breath away."

How could she not admire such a person who cares and takes the time with patience for her introspection? "If I was a grunter, I would now grunt."

He laughed. "Go ahead. It won't hurt you."

She had to force it but grunted. "So, Elliot, I really don't have to tell you what matters now and later because it all matters."

"You said it. Do you believe it?"

"Now I do."

"Good. We are making progress. There is a classic story about a professor who was teaching a course in existentialism. When it came to the final exam, he placed a chair on the front desk and told the students who had the examination booklets in front of them to prove that the chair does not exist. They all started writing furiously. After two minutes, one student came up and turned his paper in. All of the other students wrote until the bell at the end of the hour sounded. When the grades were posted, only one student received an A. It was the student who turned in his paper right away. His booklet had only two words written in it – What chair?"

"I get it."

"I knew you would, with or without a grunt."

Maddie laughed. "I need to get home to walk my dog and then to return these books to their rightful place."

"Their rightful place is wherever they are."

Walking home, Maddie had one overriding thought. If Elliott's son had not died, he would have been the person for her to love.

Though leaves are many, the root is one;
Through all the lying days of my youth
I swayed my leaves and flowers in the sun;
Now I may wither into the truth.

— William Butler Yeats

TWENTY-FIVE

Two days later a light snow filled the air. As Maddie made her way to the Library, it was evident how Elliott had inspired her to be observant and to study all of the surroundings. She noticed things she had seen before but had not questioned or remembered. She thought about their place and purpose in the scheme of things. It was a play changer. No wonder students flocked to his classes.

When she arrived at her office, a middle-aged woman was sitting on the bench by the door. When she stood, Maddie observed she was quite tall and even through the coat she wore it was evident she had broad shoulders. The woman was not what one would describe as attractive although her sharp features were classical and interesting. What was even more intriguing was that the woman was holding a magnificent plant in an earthen container. Her voice was husky yet refined. "You have to be Maddie. I would have guessed even without your name on the door."

Maddie smiled. "I must be."

The woman smiled, revealing straight white teeth. "I am Dee, Deena Poindexter, Elliott's wife."

"This is a pleasant surprise. Please come into the office."

Both women took off their coats and hung them on the hall tree standing in the corner. Dee placed the plant on the desk. "Elliott hasn't stopped talking about you. I have not seen him this excited about a youngster. I just dropped him off and just had to come meet you and thank you for the attention you are showing him."

"As you probably know better than I do, I am the one who is

benefiting by him just talking to me. He is a fascinating person."

"Ah, he is my special treasure."

"Please sit down."

"This plant is for you. I raise plants and flowers. This is a hearty indoor plant, and all you have to do is water it once a week and it will thrive with or without much light."

"It is beautiful. Thank you. I was raised in New York City, and while plants and flowers appeal to me they are alien in my frame of reference."

"Just what I would expect a librarian to say. My family had an extensive nursery. I was raised in that culture and love them. I have lush summer gardens at the house and Elliott had a commercial sized hothouse built in the back for me so I can garden all year long."

"I know what a hothouse is but I have never been in one."

"Then you must come and visit and I will give you a tour. For the full flower gardens you will have to come again in the Spring and Summer."

"Mighty kind of you. I certainly would enjoy that. Have you been in the Library before?"

"Just back when I was briefly a student."

"Would you like me to show you the inner workings?"

"Sure. Thank you."

Maddie took Dee around, and the two women talked the entire time. Maddie could tell from the many things Dee said about Elliott that she cared for him deeply. Before she left, Dee did not hold back on the history of meeting and marrying him. Each year Elliott hired one of the students in his classes to be his research assistant and to live in the house with him to drive him back and forth to the college as well as aid him in physical maneuvers and the chores of the household. Each time it had been a male student basically because there was the need for physical strength to meet the demands of getting him in and out of the wheelchair and with other functions. No female had ever applied. When Dee did apply and he saw how tall and strong she was and had even been a discus thrower in high school, he figured he would give her a chance. It turned out to be a perfect match. She was up to all of the physical demands and displayed an uncanny knowledge about the inner workings of philosophy. Taking care of the house and grounds were easy for her. He was mesmerized by her sincere attention, as well as her inquisitive nature and sharp wit. It did not take long for the two to become dependent on each other. Dee withdrew as a student to care for him full time, take care of the house, and tend to the gardens. Elliott loved his gentle giant. Affection and tenderness filled the painful void, and he promised her a hothouse if she married him. She would have married him without that promise as she loved him. Dee had been seeking a purpose in life, and without any doubt this was it. She expected and wanted no more. She participated more in his academic life, and the mutual working relationship further solidified the unusual life they had together. Perhaps it could not be adequately explained and might be puzzling to others, yet it made perfect sense to them. The age and physical differences were inconsequential. For Maddie, it was a love story for the ages.

Dee put her coat on and the two women hugged. After Dee left Maddie stared at the plant. Its beauty and sturdiness represented the love story she had just heard. It also was a symbol of her own romantic destiny.

Love has gone and left me and I don't know what to do;
This or that or what you will is all the same to me;
But all the things that I begin I leave before I am through, –
There's little use in anything as far as I can see.

— Edna St. Vincent Millay

TWENTY-SIX

At times, one mystifying aspect of life arises with new options and fresh opportunities. Maddie was thinking that it would be best not to be included in the Saturday night dinners with Marie and now Sy. It was awkward, and she had the feeling that the couple wanted to be alone and probably deserved to be. How to get out of it without hurting feelings or ruffling feathers was the dilemma. The dilemma solved itself when Dee stopped by the next day after dropping Elliott off. "I wanted to check on the plant and to invite you to dinner at our house on Saturday."

"I would be delighted, but I don't have a car."

"It's much too far to walk in this cold weather and in the dark. Write out your address and I will pick you up around five. That will give me enough time to show you the hothouse before we eat."

"Thank you."

Marie sounded genuinely disappointed when Maddie telephoned her with the news that she was invited to Professor Poindexter's for dinner on Saturday. "It won't be the same without you. I will suffer from French withdrawal, so we will have to arrange another form of get-together."

Dee gave Maddie a tour of the house, at least the first floor where they actually lived. It was an old Tudor house and there was a handicap ramp leading up the front steps. The home had plenty of character, including wood paneling and many books shelves jammed with books. Any empty space on shelves or on furniture was occupied with what she was told were antiques. Beyond a large formal dining room, which served also as a workplace with the table made to accommodate a wheelchair, was an oversized kitchen with updated appliances. She was told that they never used the second floor but that it had two bedrooms and a full bathroom.

Then came the tour of the hothouse, and it was hot and humid with pungent smells. Maddie just assumed plants loved such a home. Different levels of wooden stands were occupied with a host of plants and flowers of varying shapes and colors. Orchids were cited as an example by Dee of a flower with thousands of species. Avid collectors traveled the world over to obtain a new or elusive variety. One was actually found to be growing out of a crack in a cliff.

Elliott was apparently well rested and in a jovial mood. While Dee made final preparations for dinner in the kitchen, he told Maddie some humorous stories about his students and showed her a few antiques that had intriguing stories behind them. While Maddie offered to help, Dee was well accustomed to functioning in the kitchen by herself and, as Elliott described, completely competent to do anything perfectly if she put her mind to it. Besides, Dee preferred that Maddie keep Elliott company.

Maddie had brought a bottle of French wine, but the hosts did not imbibe. They offered to open it for her but she told them just to hold on to it. She made a mental note that if ever invited back she would bring cookies or the like.

The Poindexters were pescatarians. They did not eat meat but did have fish. Dee made onion soup, a vegetable stew, and followed by cheese cake. Maddie enjoyed every morsel, and the accompanying conversation was stimulating. The loving words and gestures between the hosts was also very much appreciated by her romantic nature. A warm heart warms the entire being.

After dinner, they sat in the living room before a blazing fire in the massive fireplace. Elliott could not contain the following remark. "Old people, old house, new feelings. Sound familiar?"

Maddie chuckled. "Old grunts and new burps."

Dee chimed in, "Probably a private joke but I think you two are evenly matched."

Elliott filled her in on Whittier's phrase. "It probably should have been Forever old, forever new, forever near. One need not go very far to find good examples."

Dee sprang to her feet. "You are right about that. Probably the closest and clearest example is right behind the house. Flowers and plants intertwine the old constantly and perpetually with the new. Have you ever seen a new tree grow right up out of an old tree or even a tree stump after the tree has been cut down?"

Elliott gestured with a waving hand. "Very appropriate, my sweet." He continued after a hesitation for a grunt. "Probably the best example is a rainbow. I have, as you know, a special affinity for rainbows. They have probably been around since the first rain, although the scientific cause didn't come until 1304 by the German monk, Theodori. Yet, each time one appears, it is as if it is for the first time. With luck you can see a double rainbow. You can't get newer than that"

Maddie had to think for a moment, but it then came to her clearly. "Rainbows find their way in poetry. I remember part of the 1802 Wordsworth poem My Heart Leaps Up:

My heart leaps up when I behold
A rainbow in the sky:
So was it when my life began,
So it is now I am a man
So be it when I shall grow old,
Or let me die!

"Right on the money, little lady. Now, tell us about your poetry."

"You mean the poetry I dabble at. It is a form of release, a diversion. I am a romantic at heart, and the feelings swell up inside of me. Since I have read the great poets as a youngster this is the form my expressions take."

Not unexpectedly, Elliott grunted. Maybe, it was a burp. "Do you share such masterpieces?"

"Not usually. Since you have shared part of your lives with me, I will share accordingly. Watching and appreciating what you two have inspires me to do more."

"What you have seen and heard here," Elliott spoke slowly, "Is for you only. We have kept our lives as private as possible and want to keep it that way."

"I understand and it is no problem for me. I will honor your wishes."

"Good. Now tell us something that two old sticks-in-the-mud can latch on to."

"Now I know why I was invited. Don't you have television?"

Elliott grunted. "There is nothing like live entertainment."

Dee added lightly, "We need a young mind flashback so we can remember what it was like."

"Me, too," Maddie smiled. "But since Elliott knows I have an undaunted curiosity about dreams, I will tell you about the unsettling dream I had last night. The most amazing part is that it startled me awake twice, and when I fell back to sleep the dream picked up where it had left off when I awoke."

"Ah," Elliott rumbled, "What I call a serial dream."

"I was in a large banquet room in a swanky hotel. It was a poetry publishers conference soliciting poetry for publication. Each publisher had a table, and there were long lines at each table. It was very crowded, very noisy, nearly unruly. Lots of shoving and other rude behavior. I had a portfolio of my poems with me. I was very tired and the wait time was long. My legs ached and I was very thirsty and there was nothing to drink anywhere. At the first table that I finally got up to, the man at the table gave me a stern look, almost one of contempt. Before I could show him my portfolio, he asked if I was already a published poet. When I said no, he said harshly that he was therefore not interested in my work and I should get out of the line. At the second table, again after a long and agonizing wait, a matronly woman asked me if my poems rhyme. When I said yes, she shouted she was not interested in looking at them. Totally frustrated, I decided I would try one more line and if I received the same kind of treatment I would give up and go home. After another long wait, an erratic woman tried to cut in before me. I wouldn't let her in. The crowd around me started screaming at me as well as pushing me to let her in because the woman was sickly. One man banged my arm and I dropped the portfolio and papers scattered all over. I had to get out of line to gather them up. The people in line would not let me get back in. A young man who had bent down to help me pick up the papers disappeared into the crowd with the papers he had collected. I yelled out but was completely ignored. When I awoke the last time I was sweating and shaking."

Dee came over and hugged her. "Poor thing. I am fortunate in that my dreams, which I rarely remember, are simple and stress free."

Elliott grunted. "Seems to me a reflection of your conscience doing battle over whether or not you should try to get your poems published. It looks like the not was prevailing."

Maddie sighed. "Sounds reasonable, but no rewind, please."

For the next hour they talked about many different things, the conversation lively and interesting. Dee drove her home.

Hugging Blizzard closely, Maddie thought about the evening. She had enjoyed it immensely and felt completely at ease with the unusual couple. They were easy to love.

Dreaming as the days go by,
Dreaming as the summers die;
Ever drifting down the stream - -
Lingering in the golden dream - -
Life, what is it but a dream?

— Lewis Carroll

TWENTY-SEVEN

It was on Wednesday when Dee telephoned Maddie. "We so enjoyed having you. Elliott and I would love to have you for dinner every Saturday except when you have a date with some young fella."

"Fat chance of that! I had such a good time that there is no way I can turn down such a wonderful idea. I hate for you to have to pick me up so often. I am going to have a friend teach me how to drive, and once I have my license I am going to buy a car."

"That sounds like a good idea in general. I don't mind the driving. I do take Elliott to and from every day, but you do what you think is best for you. You are the most level-headed person I have ever known."

As soon as she hung up the telephone, Maddie called Will. He said he would teach her in exchange for a date. Maddie told him she would see, figuring she could talk him out of the date idea when the time came. Besides, it took only a couple of lessons for Maddie to conquer that unknown.

There were a series of congenial Saturday night dinners at the Poindexters and an occasional one at Maddie's place. Each get together was exhilarating emotionally and intellectually. Maddie looked forward to each of these weekly events. Behind what others might perceive as tough exteriors, Maddie knew the couple was warm and loving. It is too bad society perceives the notion that people who want to be private as being secretive to the point that they have something to hide. More and more the sense of family surrounded the trio. Maddie shared her poetry with them, and Elliott let Maddie read the first draft of the new book he was working on with Dee. Dee showed Maddie all of the ways to tend to the plants and flowers, and they worked the gardens together. Maddie liked to boast that for a city girl she had become countryfied, or at the least was having a communion with Nature. She loved working in the dirt and watching the beauty of growth.

Over the Summer Maddie went to Paris to visit her parents for two weeks. Dee kept Blizzard, and by the time she returned the woman and dog were well bonded. Even Elliott liked having the quiet and gentle dog around, and Blizzard took all of the grunts in stride.

If nothing else, Maddie's first year at Blantyre had been interesting. She had ably settled into a job she was good at and loved. She had been involved in a couple of mysteries, one leading her to view her first dead body. She had become acquainted with a host of interesting people, associations that helped her further understand the vagaries of life and emotions as well as contributing to making her a more sensitive and caring person. A loveable canine had become a faithful companion. She had learned to drive and now owned a car. Above all else she had gotten close to an unusual loving couple that gave her an ever expanding sense of family. For a young person embarking on the greatest adventure of all.......life, it meant a great deal. Before leaving for France all of these feelings swelled up in her and inspired her to commit them to verse.

Embarking on a trip down life's highway,
A road not charted or traveled by anyone;
Not even sure if there are tolls one has to pay,
And having no idea when the venture might be done;
Smooth pavement or hazards not warned in any book,
Fair skies or storms affecting progress,
Unknown stops either a danger or a scenic overlook;
When to accelerate or slow down only a guess;
Little chance to go back or redo a part,

No comfort that others battle the same design;
Boldly to go forward with a brave heart,
And a sign that says this trip is mine.

On the flight back from Paris, Maddie eagerly looked forward to a new school year. Unlike her first year filled with so many uncertainties, she had the confidence of experience. The bedrock for her rising edifice was established by people who cared about her and who loved her. She was certain there was nothing she could not accomplish.

BOOK THREE

Designation and Resignation

In the Morning of Life

In the morning of life, when its cares are unknown,
And its pleasures in all their new lustre begin,
When we live in a bright-beaming world of our own,
And the light that surrounds us is all from within;
Oh 'tis not, believe me, in that happy time
We can love, as in hours of less transport we may; - -
Of our smiles, of our hopes 'tis the gay sunny prime,
But affection is truest when these fade away.

When we see the first glory of youth pass us by,
Like a leaf on the stream that will never return,
When our cup, which had sparkled with pleasure so high,
First tastes of the other, the dark-flowing urn;
Then, then in the time when affection holds sway
With a depth and tenderness joy never knew;
Love, nursed among pleasures, is faithless as they,
But the love born of Sorrow, like Sorrow, is true.

In climes full of sunshine, though splendid with flowers,
Their sighs have no freshness, their odour no worth;
'Tis the cloud and the mist of our own Isle of showers
That call the rich spirit of fragrancy forth,
So it is not 'mid splendour, prosperity, mirth,
That the depth of Love's generous spirit appears;

Daniel Hill Zafren

To the sunshine of smiles it may first owe its birth,
But the soul of its sweetness is drawn out by tears.

— Thomas Moore

TWENTY-EIGHT

Maddie stood before the large oak door. She stared at the block letters set on the wood: *M. Ponte, Head Librarian.* It was difficult to believe that she had been at Blantyre University for nine years, that six years ago she had been promoted to Assistant Head Librarian, and a year ago made Head Librarian when Constance Gilford retired. She was a natural choice for the position because of her librarian skills, her working knowledge of the collections, her energy and enthusiasm, and her professional managerial style.

She entered the office and closed the door behind her. She settled in the plush chair at the desk, and after checking the plant which Dee had given her so many years ago and which traveled to each office she had been in and now occupied almost half of this desk, she swiveled around and looked out the picture window to the campus. It was a sunny spring day, the grass had turned green, the trees were budding, and birds were plentiful. She thought about all that had transpired over these nine years, cataloging them as a librarian is prone to do.

At the end of that first school year, Sy had been offered the job as Editor for the American Legal Bulletin, a weekly national legal newspaper based in San Francisco. It was a good opportunity for him. Marie went with him to finish her book and for them to remain together. They married a year later. Marie, teaching English in a high school, sent Maddie frequent emails to keep her informed of their activities.

Marie's book, *Addressee Unknown*, lay on her desk next to the plant. Maddie turned from viewing the campus and picked up the book which she did often. It was a way of thinking about and being close to a special friend. She also believed that the book was replete with wisdom and common sense for those of the younger generation floundering or unsure of their destiny or the future of mankind. She would recommend it to students who came to her office for research assistance who would start a conversation on how difficult it was to grow up in this day and age. She also had a bookmark at her favorite place in the book, although it was an excerpt that Marie had quoted from another author. Early on when Maddie had told Marie about Daniel Hill Zafren's spellbinding mystery, Marie had looked him up and discovered that he had written a number of books besides the mystery, most dealing with the lessons of life. She ordered a couple of them, and totally was absorbed by them. She ordered the rest of them, and after reading them all contacted him in person to exchange ideas, many of which worked their way into her undertaking. When she asked him if she could use a quote by him of his philosophy first stated in his book *In A World We Never Made* and repeated in later books, he graciously agreed. That excerpt was so compatible with Maddie's own outlook, refined by the many discussions with Elliott, that she read it often as a comforting reinforcement of her own being. She picked up the book, opened it to the marked site and read it anew.

When all is said and done, even though it is a world we never made, that does not mean we have to accept it as it is. We can work with and for others to change it. Perhaps, not completely or all at once, but it can be done. A Japanese proverb conjures up an appropriate image:

Even a mountain can be worn away by the tread of many feet.

There is also the possibility of making a special place within or just for ourselves. A warm, inviting niche to allow us to think without limitations, to feel without inhibitions, to exist without criticism or rebuke by others. A space reserved for the inner self to rise to the surface and to elevate to a plateau from which all can be observed and understood without outside influences. A safe, secure and congenial mental and emotional fortress. A place called home.

Upon receiving his degree, Will went to work in the Forensic Division of the Federal Bureau of Investigation in Washington, D.C. He married a file clerk he met there and they had two sons. Maddie received a telephone call from him a few times a year, and he was still proud of their friendship.

Harry's sons became lawyers and were working for the same Wall Street law firm. His daughter passed through the University receiving a degree in Sociology. No longer in need of the free tuition offered by the college, Harry retired and started to write a mystery novel. He was further inspired to do so by Daniel Hill Zafren's sequel to *Network of Death* entitled *Network Secret*, and he was amazed that the author could produce a sequel as compelling as the original book. Harry's effort, as yet unfinished, started with the same kind of puzzling suicide that they had known about where the identity of the person was never established and no one had ever reported him missing. To this day Maddie still could not make full sense of that development.

Honore graduated and after that Maddie never heard from or about her. She had stopped by at random times over the school years to see if Maddie had changed her mind, but the visits were brief and became less frequent in the face of a cool reception.

As Maddie had predicted, eight years ago Sally left her African involvement and returned to the United States. She found a job as the Assistant Director at a no-kill animal shelter in South Carolina. Three years later she rose to the Director position, and she added as a function of the organization for it to be a national advocate for animal welfare.

Four years ago Elliott died after a brief illness. Dee and Maddie were deeply saddened by his absence. He had been a source of goodness and reason for them, and it is heart-wrenching to lose one you love. The two women comforted each other. Even though his abbreviated closing days were filled with pain and medicines made him drowsy, Elliott somehow managed to write short letters to Dee and Maddie. After his funeral and the memorial service at the University where thousands paid tribute to a great mind, they opened the letters and shared them with each other.

My precious Dee:

All that I write here will not be a surprise to you as I have told you these things repeatedly, and deservedly so. Thank you for all you have done for me and have been for me. I love you very much. Emerging from a void in my life, I managed to become part of a person by losing myself in teaching and writing. Then you came along, a bright and warm light piercing my darkness. Your love, concern, and tenderness added a new life to me and for which I am so grateful. You are my gentle giant, and I take to my grave the thoughts and warm loving memories of you.

I was worried about leaving you alone. Then Maddie magically entered our lives and I know you will not be alone. I love you to my last breath.

Your Elliott

My dear Maddie:

You know, as I have told you often enough, that I

consider you and love you as my daughter. From a time when I never thought I could be happy, I discovered a new happiness with Dee. You added to that happiness greatly.

The year after the accident has been a time I have never talked about except to Dee. As there is a lesson in it, I want to also share it with you. I stayed in a small guest house in the mountains of North Carolina run by an elderly gentleman who had also lost his wife in a tragic accident. A mutual silence brought solace to us both. I had thought there was nothing left for me in this world, but the peace there brought about a basic will to go on as best as I could. Early one morning at the year's end, before a storm approached, from the porch I was mesmerized by a beautiful rainbow. It was such a magnificent sight that I wanted more, and I reasoned that if I could want more of that I could want more for myself. I kept a picture of a rainbow in my office to remind me of this. Be steadfast, my daughter, and do not ever be afraid to dream and live life to the fullest. I just know that you will find and have all that you deserve. My special love remains there with you.

Elliott

The women cried and hugged tightly. Dee had the years they had together to fall back on, and Elliott had the foresight to make her the beneficiary of the life insurance policy and pension through the University. Maddie hoped that she could be as strong a person as Dee was. Dee decided to stay in the house where the memories were as well as the hothouse and gardens. About six months after his death, Dee proposed to Maddie that she move into the house with her. Maddie could have the entire second floor to herself and they would share kitchen chores. Since over the years they had become very close and Maddie considered Dee her United States mother, she accepted the generous offer. Dee had taught her so much about gardening, Maddie was further enticed to be there so she could fully participate in that endeavor, a very enjoyable task performed together.

Some six months after moving to the house Blizzard died from an inoperable cancerous tumor in her chest. She had lost much of her quality of life and the only humane act was to put her to sleep. It was a difficult and heart draining decision. Even though in the house for a short time Blizzard loved to run through the garden pathways. They buried her in a vacant place towards the back of the gardens. A few months later they adopted two mixed terriers from the shelter, a brother and sister, who had been abandoned. It did not take long for this pair to become an integral part of the combined household.

Maddie's parents had aged but were in good health. They were not in shape to make the trip to the United States so Maddie went to visit them twice a year, over Christmas and for two weeks during the summer. Maddie liked to engage them in conversations about her childhood as she wanted to remember all of those sweet days. The visits were warm and relaxing, and there was still a lingering love for Paris which would probably always be in her blood.

Maddie was, as she liked to phrase it, at a strange place in her life's journey. She was basically happy, primarily because her job was so challenging and satisfying. Dee's pleasant mannerism, company, and sage counsel, contributed to her mental and emotional well being. Her thirty-first birthday was coming up, and the realization that she had yet to find fulfillment of her love interest and that the healthy child bearing age was slipping away, gave her some degree of concern. There had been few dates and opportunities for romance. Yet, she was resigned to the life she had. It was not entirely what she had hoped for, and whispered dreams were carried off by daily currents. As Elliott advised in the letter she would not give up entirely on her dreams, a thought echoed by Dee. Above and beyond all that she had, and she did have a great deal to be grateful for, something wonderful might be just beyond the next curve in the road. A romantic does not desert the ship even if it is not as seaworthy as it used to be and vital parts are getting rusty. Her life's vessel can still carry her across fair or stormy seas. A rainbow might appear at any time. Whatever the future might hold, she would greet it and accept it, and make the most of it. Above all else, it would be forever old and forever new.